BOOKS BY E.M. SMITH
The Agent Juliet series
Broken Bones

BOOKS BY TIM MCBAIN & L.T. VARGUS
Casting Shadows Everywhere
The Awake in the Dark series
The Scattered and the Dead series
The Clowns
The Violet Darger series

BEYOND GOOD & EVIL

BEYOND
GOOD & EVIL

A VICTOR LOSHAK NOVEL

E.M. SMITH
L.T. VARGUS & TIM MCBAIN

BEYOND
GOOD & EVIL

PROLOGUE

Coffee lurched against the inside of the Go Gators mug as Stan Murphy shuffled through his front door. He hesitated there, eased the door shut behind him, and stepped onto his screened-in front porch, one eye locked on the scalding liquid sloshing around.

In the near-darkness of the early morning, the coffee was a solid black that slopped and rolled like a mini sea in an invisible hurricane, but none of the waves made it over the flood walls. They never did. He might not be moving as fast as he did when he was a young buck, but even at eighty-one years old, he had compensation like a damn gyroscope.

A breath of cool morning air caused Stan's skin to pucker all down his arms and back. Weatherman on Channel 7 said it was going to be a hot one today — 96 and muggy as a sweaty crotch — but in this hour before dawn, the humid breeze put a chill in his bones.

Well, it couldn't be helped. Stan groaned as he lowered himself onto the swing, legs and back creaking, but still not spilling a drop of coffee. Cold breeze or not, if he didn't get out there first thing in the morning, there wouldn't be anybody to protect his lawn from those putrid little shits down the block. Riding their bikes across it, dragging their heels through it, tearing up all that lovely green sod like fucking heathens when there was a perfectly good sidewalk right there! Bullshit was what it was. Parents not beating

1

their kids enough, letting the little thugs terrorize the whole neighborhood. By God, if he'd pulled that kind of crap when he was their age, you'd better believe there would've been consequences. None of this namby-pamby Jimmy or Jenny or whoever didn't *mean* to, Mr. Murphy, surely it isn't that big of a *deal*, Mr. Murphy, they're just *kids*, Mr. Murphy.

Stan took a sip of his coffee, the hot, bitter liquid fighting off a measure of the chill. Vandalism, that was what it was. Didn't matter how old they were.

He gave the porch swing an easy push with the toes of his house shoes and let the sway carry off the familiar rant. He'd made it outside before anybody else woke up. He had his cordless phone in the pocket of his bathrobe, ready to call the cops on any little miscreant who took a notion today.

Stan leaned his back against the wooden slats of the porch swing and drank his coffee as gray leeched into the blue-black sky overhead. Soon the pole lights all down the block would wink out, and another fiery orange Florida sunrise would vanquish the gauzy gray shroud.

Wouldn't be long now, folks would start stirring around. Getting ready for work and school. Stan craned his neck toward the gray two-story a few houses down, the home of the most frequent offenders. The Nicholsons. Tom and Margie were good people. She brought him meals sometimes, and Tom always stopped to ask him how the Gators were doing, but they didn't know shit about raising kids. Into all that sensitive New-age baloney, and it showed — their yard was a disaster area. Bike tracks across the grass, ugly brown grooves, and one time he'd seen their youngest digging a hole in it with a damned spoon.

Looking at the Nicholson lawn now in the early morning light, something seemed more offensive than usual.

Not just ugly. Wrong.

Gray rectangles lay strewn across the grass.

Were they frames? Stan set his coffee on the porch railing and pushed himself to his feet, his joints protesting. It looked like all the screens had been ripped out of their windows and thrown around. From this far away, he couldn't tell whether the edges were bent or tore-up, but he couldn't imagine a guy like Tom doing late night construction.

Stan shuffled out the porch's screen door and down his steps onto the walk to get a better view.

From that angle, he could see the Nicholson's door was open. Not wide. Just a touch. Something about that thin strip of black between the door and the jamb made him uneasy. It was almost suggestive, like parted lips.

"Uh."

The sound was more an exhalation of air as it left his throat, an admission of uncertainty. Something was wrong. The door should be open wide or shut all the way, not in between.

He fumbled to pull the cordless from his pocket. In the gray light, he could just barely read the number for Tom's cell phone on the back. He had Tom's and Margie's. *Just in case*, Margie said when she wrote them down for him. Meaning, *Just in case you slip and break your hip, old man.* Not, *Just in case our door's hanging open a little ways, and you don't know what to do, old man.*

But that door. It wasn't right.

Stan punched in Tom's number and lifted the phone to his ear, listening to the ring. When Tom answered, Stan would say, "Sorry to wake you up, but did you know your front door's open for God and everybody to look inside?" Something casual like that. And Tom would yawn and say something along the lines of, "Oh, one of the kids probably left it open."

The ringing stopped. Stan opened his mouth to say the predetermined lines.

"You have reached the voice mailbox of [Tom Nicholson]. Please leave a message after the beep."

No reason to get bent out of shape, Stan told himself. Tom probably kept his phone in the kitchen while he slept. Yeah, he'd probably been on his way to pick it up, tripping over toys and junk, and just didn't make it before the answering machine picked up. He would give Tom a second to get to his phone, then call back.

Stan hung up and started down the sidewalk almost absently, trying not to think about the sweat moistening his armpits and prickling in the crack of his ass. When he made it to the Nicholson's mailbox, he hit Redial.

After a couple buzzing rings from the earpiece, Stan's hearing aide picked up something else. A shrill, brassy music, almost painful in the otherwise relative silence of the street.

Tom's ringtone.

It was coming from inside the house.

His skin broke out in goose bumps, and a shiver ran down his stooped spine.

"You have reached the voice mailbox of—"

Stan hung up and stared at the slit of blackness between the door and the jamb. Earlier he'd thought the opening was small, just cracked a little. Now that void seemed to take up his entire field of vision.

He twisted the cordless in his hands. Someone should've answered. With all that racket going on, there was no way Tom and Margie and their kids wouldn't have heard it.

So, what? Should he call the cops? Stan swallowed hard, forcing the spit down past the dry lump in his throat. Yeah, call the cops was exactly what he would do.

But his worn house slippers started walking up the steps to their door. The weathered wood planks bent under his soles, moaning a little. His heart stuttered against the inside of his chest as he pushed the door the rest of the way open.

It swung away from him without a sound, a gray rhombus of light leaning in around him and illuminating the house's innards. A hall table under a mirror. A carpeted staircase.

He stepped inside, but his foot landed wrong. The floor sort of squished and turned, twisting his ankle as it pitched him off.

Falling.

Stan gasped and cried out. Watched the floor rushing up to clobber him.

His gnarled hands flew out in front just in time, the heels of his palms slamming against the corner of a stair, shooting bright jags of pain up his arms and into his back. Jolting. Stabbing. But his wrists miraculously didn't snap.

His phone thudded over the carpet, then clattered onto the hardwood. It rocked back and forth on its rounded back, slowly going still. And the silence of the place thrust itself at him again. Hollow and ominous.

Red lights bounced around the hall in a weird flickery dance. All Stan could think of were twirling police lights, but they weren't right. He knew they weren't right.

As he pushed himself back upright, he followed the lights back to their source — a tiny child's shoe with lights in the sole.

He wiped a hand across his mouth, suddenly ashamed of yelling. Just a damn shoe. It'd been left in the middle of the hall, and along he'd come and tripped over it like some bumbling old fart.

"Tom?" He grimaced at the weak, frightened sound of his voice. Like some kind of newborn kitten. He cleared his throat and tried again.

"Tom? Margie?"

Silence answered him.

Stan wiped a shaky hand across the whiskers on his upper lip, brushing away a sheen of sweat. It was warm inside, the house holding onto yesterday's heat for dear life.

Slowly, his twisted ankle throbbing, Stan padded through the living room and into the kitchen. A pinprick of blue light blinked at him from the counter. Tom's phone.

Stan edged past, toward the hallway. He'd been over for Thanksgiving last year. Knew the bathroom was down that way, just before you got to the master bedroom.

"Hello?" he hollered down the dark hall.

No response.

He sidled into the darkness, eyes locked on the bedroom door at the end of the hall. Light poked out around the edges, gray with a touch of orange. Seeing it made him feel inexplicably better, like he'd been wandering through a dark forest and stumbled upon a welcoming campfire. He picked up the pace.

His hand settled on the door, trembling and grizzled-looking in the gray-orange light. Old. Weak. His pulse accelerated again, pounding in his throat as he turned the knob and pushed.

"Tom, your front door's standing wide open—"

The door stopped short with a soft thud.

"Tom?"

Stan poked his head through the crack to see what was blocking the door.

That gray-orange light streamed down through the skylights, illuminating the whole bedroom in predawn color.

A body lay in the door's path, a thinning head of hair resting against the bottom, stopping it from opening all the way. It took several seconds before Stan realized it was Tom. Facedown. Arms folded under his chest awkwardly. The carpet around him dark and soggy with blood.

Eyes wide, mouth opening and shutting convulsively, Stan raised his head to the bed as if to ask Margie what happened.

She lay sprawled across a wet, red comforter, naked, her legs open wide. Smears covered Margie's body where bloody hands had touched her. Groped her.

Sightless eyes bulged in her skull, bulbous and full of fright. And beneath that, her lips were pulled back in a frozen snarl, tongue lolling out of one side.

Her head canted at an odd angle, neck extended and

bent too far back. Purple rings lined her throat. Dark, angry-looking stripes against the pale skin.

A sudden heat pounded in Stan's temples, embarrassed for her, for seeing her like this. Then a wave of cold chased it from his body: *The kids.*

All thought fled, taking with it the aches and pains of age, as Stan dashed down the hall, back through the kitchen and living room to the staircase. His old joints creaked and cracked as he sprinted up the steps. He'd never been up there before, too hard on his knees, so he wasn't sure which room the kids slept in, but he went on anyway, hell-bent on finding them.

Finding them alive, by God. *Alive.* The word was the only coherent thing he could cling to.

The first door on his left had princess stickers stuck to the jamb. He wrenched it open.

The little girl slumped in the corner, her pastel green pajamas marred by a streak of red stretching down from a gaping hole in her neck, a wound so deep and dark that he couldn't even see the bottom of it. Flaps of ragged flesh hung along its sides. Torn.

The blood was everywhere. All over the carpet, spattered down the side of the toybox, the walls, on the sheets. Then he realized the boy was down there, half sticking out from beneath the bunk bed as if he'd tried to crawl under and hide.

Tom Junior. The name came to Stan in a flash, and he realized the boy had died face-down, just like his father.

A strangled sob made Stan jump, and he took an instinctive step backward, eyes darting from the girl — wasn't it Jenny? — to the boy, searching for signs of life.

But no, they were gone. Dead. The sound had been him. Tears coursed down Stan's cheeks, the awful sounds accompanying them. It felt like the sobs were being torn up from the bottom of his stomach.

He wasn't sure how he made it down the stairs, but he knew he was outside when the oppressive heat of that house gave way and cold, wet air surrounded him. He stumbled over the curb, across the asphalt.

Green grass filled his vision. His perfect lawn.

He hunched over, hands on his knees, and vomited coffee all over the sod.

CHAPTER 1

Victor Loshak crossed the parking lot toward the academy classrooms, his briefcase swinging lightly at his side, a cup of coffee he'd snagged from McDonald's in the opposite hand. Steam curled from the open hole and disappeared into the chilly fall day. He hadn't taken a drink yet, but he knew what he'd find on that first sip. Watered-down. Weak. Hot water with coffee flavoring. Still, it beat gas station coffee. No matter what "blend" each cannister claimed to be, whatever you got always tasted like the chemicals they used to clean the machines every night.

An overcast day like today demanded the comfort of a hot brew in the hand, burning the taste buds and sliding down into the gut, and the McDonald's on Russel had been the only handy drive-thru on his way to class.

Overhead, the sky was gunsmoke gray broken up by wisps of slightly darker stuff the shade of concrete, and threatening showers.

The thought of cold rain made him crave the scalding brown liquid, so he took a drink. No surprises there. The stuff was offensive in its inoffensiveness. The best thing that could be said about it was that it would probably stay hot for another twenty minutes before it cooled to lukewarm territory and he'd have to gulp what was left. That would get him through the first couple slides of his lecture at least.

Loshak took another sip as he stepped up onto the

sidewalk.

In his breast pocket, his phone began to vibrate. An irrational part of him hoped it would be Darger, but when he slipped the smartphone out of his jacket, he didn't recognize the number. He swiped the answer icon.

"Loshak."

"Hello, Agent. This is Jevon Spinks. Crime reporter out of Miami. I'd like to talk to you about a series of murders taking place down this way. "

The word *reporter* triggered warning bells. Loshak noted, half-amused, that he stood up straighter, made himself seem bigger as if to assert his dominance. He could even feel his brows come together in a grim line.

"I haven't heard anything about these murders, so I can't comment," he said. Short, clipped. His no-dicking-around voice as his partner would've said. Probably former partner, soon.

He was already lowering the phone from his ear, his thumb approaching the red icon to disconnect when the reporter shouted, "Wait, I'm not digging for a quote!" as if he could see Loshak trying to hang up.

Spinks rushed on without taking a breath, "This guy massacred a whole family in their beds last night — mom, dad, two kids. One of the victims was a six-year-old girl. The killer cut her throat so deeply that he chipped his knife on her vertebra. And the Nicholson family is just the latest in this string. I've linked a total of three home invasion murders across the Dade-Broward-Palm Beach jurisdictions to this killer. The cops here are chasing their tails. Tripping all over each other. Nobody knows what anybody else knows, nobody's talking to anybody—"

"Have you tried reaching out to the local FBI field office?" Loshak nodded to a pair of cadets passing by on their way to his lecture. "They can form up a task force and start getting the communication process between the departments streamlined."

On the other end of the line, Spinks chuckled. "I did contact them, and I had a lot of fun playing runaround for about eight seconds. Then it started to get old. That's why I called you. I've seen you in the papers, and I read your book on profiling by crime scene a few years back."

A drop of wetness landed on Loshak's eyelid. He blinked instinctively and headed for the shelter of the building before the sprinkles turned into a downpour.

"Then you know I mainly work serial killers, not home invasions gone wrong," he told the reporter. "I don't want to sound cold, but those are alarmingly common."

"What about serial home invasions that result in a murder or murders?" Spinks didn't leave enough of a pause for Loshak to respond. Like any good reporter, he pushed on, full steam ahead to the meat of his argument before he could be interrupted. "Ten days ago, a young woman was found dead in her home, throat slashed. Lacey Monroe. Pinecrest PD thought it was the ex-boyfriend; she took out a restraining order against him a month ago. Place was robbed, but they're going with the assumption that he took the stuff to make it look like a robbery."

"Staging the scene, yeah. Wouldn't be the first time a killer thought he was being clever that way," Loshak interjected when the reporter took a breath.

"No, it wouldn't," Spinks agreed. "Except the family I mentioned? He strangled the wife and stabbed the husband

and son so many times the coroner couldn't get a clean count. He put the official number of stab wounds at somewhere between forty and fifty. But the daughter's throat wound, that was in exactly the same style as Lacey Monroe's. And the Nicholsons were robbed, too."

Another agent on her way out held the door for Loshak. He raised his coffee to her, waving a finger in thanks. She smiled.

"And that makes you think this is a serial case," Loshak said as he stepped into the lobby, which was really more of a glorified wide spot in the hall.

A bank of elevators stood on one wall, and a stained gray couch of indeterminate material sat against the other, next to a fake plant. He knew it was fake because its leaves had failed the thumbnail test — he hadn't been able to cut it with his nail the first time he was alone with it.

"That and the fact that there was a third attack six months ago." The reporter sounded like he was really getting into this now, Peter Parker on a hot lead. "An older lady, Isabella Rodriguez, sixty-four. Raped, robbed, throat torn wide open just like the Nicholson girl and Lacey Monroe."

"Right, but you seem to think these incidents were all carried out by the same perpetrator, and I'm not seeing a connection." Loshak's voice almost echoed in the stone and glass lobby. He dropped it to a more reasonable volume. "Do you know how many rapists cut their victim's throats? It's not rare."

Spinks didn't reply right away. Loshak couldn't decide whether it was the guy's natural storytelling instinct to play up the drama of the moment, but he doubted he had convinced the reporter to drop this. You never could talk these types out of it when they believed they had something no one else had thought of.

"Well, there's an odd detail to all three scenes," Spinks finally said. "Missing silverware."

Loshak nodded to himself and rested the corner of his briefcase on the arm of the couch. "If the motive was robbery, stealing the silver wouldn't be odd at all."

"We're not talking about the real deal, Agent Loshak," the reporter said. "This was the cheap, drop thirty bucks at Walmart so your family's not eating with their hands kind of silverware."

"Huh." Loshak let his jaw hang open a little.

The elevator beeped, and the doors slid open. A few suits and a handful of cadets in khakis came out, some heading for the doors, the rest down the hall.

"How'd they even notice junk like that was missing?"

"The guy took the whole drawer with him all three times," Spinks said. "Just pulled it out of the cabinet and left."

"Huh." The word slipped out again before Loshak could stop it, but this time he didn't have any clever questions to follow it up with. Took the entire silverware drawer. A puzzle.

Then something Spinks had said near the beginning of the call came back to him.

"Profiling by crime scene. That's why you called me."

Loshak could almost see the reporter nodding in response.

"That's why I called you."

CHAPTER 2

As it turned out, the heavens never did commit to a downpour before he left Quantico, but as soon as Loshak's plane touched down in Miami that afternoon, the sky started pissing down rain.

He felt ridiculous in the terminal calling an Uber, but the guy sitting next to him on the flight had sworn up and down that it was cheaper than cab fare in Miami. Of course, the kid had been about half his age, with gauges in both ears and tattoos sticking out the bottom of his salmon cardi's pushed-up sleeves.

Loshak only felt more ridiculous when the driver pulled up in a little yellow Bug. If she was a day over seventeen, he would eat his badge. He almost asked her how long she'd had her license, but as soon as they got the pleasantries out of the way, she hit the screen of her phone, and the stereo started blaring "Here I Go Again on My Own."

Whitesnake? Jesus. He remembered when David Coverdale was still a part of Deep Purple, decades before the fetus in the driver's seat had even been born. He opened his mouth to jokingly ask her where in the world she'd ever heard of Whitesnake but snapped it back shut when he caught sight of her moving to the music. He couldn't breathe.

The girl jutted her chin out on the downbeats, over and over, like a rooster. Suddenly, she was Shelly, sticking her chin out and bopping her head, dangly hoop earrings

15

wobbling like crazy, ponytail flapping. Dressed up in shimmery Hammer pants and a tube top he'd absolutely forbidden until his wife overruled him, practicing with her little friends for some kind of ridiculous lip sync contest her middle school was putting on. Shelly had been the only one of the girls who really got into character. The rest of them couldn't stop giggling, but she rocked out straight-faced until the end.

Loshak tried to swallow, but it hurt too much. He could remember someone at the funeral — it might've even been the director — talking about how you never got over the death of your kid, you just got used to the pain. In his experience, that was utter bullshit. It'd been years and reminders that his little girl was dead still kept blindsiding him, tearing the wounds in his heart and lungs and gut open all over again. And he never fucking saw it coming.

As if she could feel his stare, the Uber driver glanced his way in the rearview.

Loshak nodded like he'd been trying to get her attention. "Yeah, about how long is it before we get to Cutler Bay?"

She turned down the music.

"We're almost definitely gonna hit traffic," she said. "So, I'd say plan for like forty-five minutes to an hour."

"Thanks."

He pulled out the file containing the information on the trio of home invasion murders and flipped it open, escaping into the relieving distance of some other family's trauma.

Everything about the murders was cringeworthy, but the rape of the retiree struck him as especially brutal. She

16

wasn't that much older than Jan, his ex-wife. He read on, reviewing the reports and photos, but his thoughts kept coming back to Jan.

He pulled his phone out and sat it on the seat by his leg. She lived down here, Jan. Moved down after the divorce. Actually, the move had been part of the reason for the divorce. She'd wanted a fresh start, somewhere far away from the house where Shelly had wasted down to jaundiced, papery skin hanging off a birdlike skeleton and finally died. But Loshak hadn't been able to go. He could've put in for a transfer to a field office somewhere, but he would've had to quit working in the BAU. Jan never said it outright, but he knew she thought he cared more about work than her. She'd never quite been able to understand that work had been all he'd had to cling to then. The only thing that kept him sane.

Staring down at the phone now, he wondered if he hadn't been selfish after all. He was a profiler, for crying out loud, he'd known how Jan was feeling. He could've told her the truth, that the weight of her grief plus his own had terrified him, and work had been the only way he could keep moving forward. He could've fought for their marriage, tried to preserve that bond. But he hadn't.

And now he was in Miami. She was, what, an hour from his hotel? Less? It would be weird if he didn't at least call her. High profile agents had a way of ending up on the news and in the papers. If she saw that, saw that he'd been right there and hadn't even bothered to call, it would end up a hell of a lot more awkward for both of them.

He picked up the phone and opened his contacts. He thumbed through until he found Jan's name but something stopped him from hitting the Call icon.

He felt suddenly nervous. Vulnerable. What if she didn't want to hear from him?

But that was stupid. A killer was running loose in the city. Surely that merited at the very least a courtesy call. If he didn't warn her and something happened, could he live with himself knowing he'd failed in that last and most important role as a husband, protecting his wife?

Probably not.

He hit Call. It rang. And kept ringing. He pictured Jan staring down at his name on her phone, trying to decide whether to answer.

More ringing. The image shifted slightly. Jan staring down at his name on the screen, then hitting the button to silence it. Staring and staring, waiting for him to take a hint and hang up already.

But Loshak didn't hang up. Maybe couldn't. He was caught up in the inertia of the call now, in the number of rings he'd already invested, the Sunk Cost Fallacy. It kept ringing, and he kept listening to it ring.

He held on until her voicemail picked up, then he thumbed the little red phone to disconnect the call. Probably just as well that she didn't answer. There was too much unresolved baggage between them for a casual chat on the phone. She knew that; it was why she hadn't answered.

Loshak slipped his phone in his pocket and turned back to the gruesome photos of the most recent crime scene, trying not to feel the twinge of disappointment in the pit of his stomach.

CHAPTER 3

The rain stopped just after Loshak dropped his bag off at the hotel, and white-hot Florida sunshine got to work turning a tolerable afternoon into a nightmare of humidity. By the time he made it to Cutler Bay, the air had congealed into a muggy, sticky soup. Just the short walk from the cab to the mailbox at the Nicholson house soaked the white shirt beneath his suit jacket and plastered his gray hair to his forehead.

A uniform from the CBPD met Loshak on the front walk. A rookie by the name of Blanton. Twenty to twenty-five. Ridiculously tall, with a knifelike Adam's apple that jumped whenever the kid swallowed.

"I have to check your badge before I can open up the house," Blanton said almost apologetically, the lump in his throat bobbing.

"No problem." Loshak gave the rookie a friendly smile and produced his badge. "Never leave home without it."

Satisfied, Blanton handed over a pair of paper booties and latex gloves, then gestured at the front door. The kid's Adam's apple could've been dicing vegetables.

Loshak wanted to say something that would put Blanton at ease as they approached the house, offer some kind of wisdom gleaned from years studying gruesome murder scenes, but he couldn't. They were about to walk into a house where a whole family had been butchered. Nothing he said would make the reality of that go down easier.

Hanging around the doorknob was one of those electronic lockboxes realtors used so they wouldn't have to carry around a key for every property. They stopped on the step, and Blanton punched in the passcode on the tiny pad. The buttons flashed green. The rookie slid open the box and took out a brass housekey.

As he unlocked the front door, he wouldn't meet Loshak's eyes.

"Didn't bring enough booties," Blanton said swinging the door open and stepping out of the way. His Adam's apple chopped at the air. "So, I'm just — uh — gonna wait out here."

"That's fine." Loshak tucked the case file under his arm, then slipped the first paper bootie over his right loafer, stepping over the threshold and setting the covered foot down inside the house. Leaning against the jamb to keep from losing his balance, he repeated the process with the left shoe.

He didn't stand back up immediately. From this angle, he could see a tiny red and blue Spiderman sneaker beneath a hall table. The sole was facing toward him. It looked almost new, no scuffing or gravel stuck in between the ridges. As if it had hardly been worn.

CSI had been all over the house. All relevant evidence would have been collected and removed to the lab, where it would be analyzed in an attempt to find the killer. All that was left behind were the bits and pieces of the victim's lives. The stuff they thought they needed and now would never come back to.

Loshak straightened up and took a few steps into the

house.

In spite of the paper booties covering his loafers, every step seemed to echo off the hardwood and bounce down the hall. It felt as if he were disturbing an empty church. Or a tomb.

The click of the door closing behind him sounded like a gunshot in all that silence. Made the hair on the back of his neck stand up, just for a second.

Loshak slipped into the living room, wanting to get the tour of the crime scene over with, but he couldn't will himself to move any faster. The quiet inside the Nicholson house demanded reverence. It was unavoidable.

In the kitchen, the hole where the stolen silverware drawer had been pulled from the cabinets gaped at him like a missing tooth. He crept across the tile to study it more closely. The cabinetry was fairly new, with the high-end slides that wouldn't let you slam anything. No bent metal or damaged stops to indicate that it had been violently ripped out. Someone had simply pulled it out, lifting at the last second to remove the wheels from their tracks.

Could be someone who worked in cabinetry, a contractor or a woodworker. Someone on an installation crew who probably hadn't stuck around long, maybe got fired for being unreliable or overly aggressive. Or it could just be someone who'd seen this sort of drawer before.

All the same, Loshak jotted down a note to check if any of the other victims had cabinets installed or repaired in the last three years.

With that done, he followed the hall down to the master bedroom, scene of the first murders.

The door stood open, and a pair of skylights overhead

flooded the room with white light. Loshak nearly had to shade his eyes from the glare.

He flipped open the file to confirm the position of the bodies. The husband had bled to death on the floor just behind the door where the widest pool of red-brown blood had dried. Multiple stab wounds to the back, chest, and face. A few defensive wounds to the hands, indicating that he'd tried to protect himself from the first few attacks, maybe even tried to fight the guy to protect his wife. Blood and tissue under the fingernails, but the lab report hadn't come back before Loshak hopped the flight. He would have to check with CSI later to see whether any of it belonged to their killer.

The wife had been found with blood and tissue under her nails as well, the odds much higher that it would be from the murderer, considering the length of time she'd been in close contact with him.

Loshak stepped over the blood pool where Tom Nicholson had died and edged around the bed where Margie Nicholson had been strangled and raped. The comforter and sheets had already been stripped and taken away as evidence, but the naked mattress remained. It sagged in the middle, one indentation large enough to fit a pair of adults, sleeping on each other's shoulder or nestled front to back, their combined weight slowly breaking down the pillowtop and springs over the years. Leaving their mark.

The window next to the bed was closed now, but in the crime scene photos, it had been open. The report noted it as the presumed entry point.

Loshak opened the file again to check the report. All the

screens on the first-floor windows ripped off. Several showed signs of tampering — scratches that might've come from a blade or screwdriver trying to pry the panes open — but the rest were all locked from the inside. This was the only window that hadn't been.

The killer had been in his right mind enough not to break the glass and wake everyone up. He'd tried all the windows on the first floor and finally found the master bedroom unlocked. Slipped inside. He would've had to kill the husband first to get him out of the way. Eliminate the threat. Fast, before the wife could escape. The depth of the stab wounds would indicate speed.

Then, his hands slippery with blood, he had raped the wife, strangling and groping, trading off hands as if he couldn't decide which part he liked more. His grip would've been sliding all over the place as he tried to choke the life from her body. Jesus knew how long it had taken, how long she had suffered.

Loshak left the dead couple's bedroom behind and headed upstairs.

The kids' room was harder to stomach. Even as long as he'd been doing this job, Loshak couldn't divorce himself emotionally from what had happened in there. He didn't think it was just because he was a father, either. Or had been one.

Children were fragile, they needed protection to survive. The social contract most of the world lived by respected that. Hell, the average Joe off the street would help a kid they'd never met if that kid was in danger, lost, or crying, whereas an adult in the same situation or worse? Tough shit. And even though Loshak had seen that social contract broken more times than he wanted to remember, there was still something gut-wrenching about standing in the room where it happened. Looking at the drying puddle of blood in the corner. The streaks of it trailing off under the bed.

This was a place where they'd felt safe, protected, where Mom and Dad left the nightlight in the corner on after kissing them goodnight. A monster had snuck in here in the middle of the night, while they were disoriented from sleep, and savaged them. Carved them up. Ended their stories with terror and pain.

It was a violation. Blasphemy.

The crime scene photos showed the tiny bodies still in their PJs, the boy's shirt shredded by the sheer number of times he'd been stabbed. First in the front, then the back, the change occurring presumably when he fell down and started to crawl away.

The girl's throat had been hacked open with a stab-slash motion that would've required her attacker to stand face-to-face with her, looking her in the eyes. No signs of rape or fondling like the mother, but there was something vaguely sexual about the method of attack. Personal. Intimate. And yet animalistic. The males of the house had been stabbed over and over again until they stopped moving, front and back and wherever was convenient, whatever it took to get them out of the way, leaving the killer alone with the females.

Loshak crouched down, knee joints clicking, and stared hard at the blood stain in the corner. Had the killer been planning to rape the daughter as well? Gotten startled into killing her and running before he could? Maybe scared away by a passing siren or the elderly neighbor who'd found the family?

No, the neighbor angle didn't fit with the timeline or the torn-off screens. The killer had come in through a window and left through the door, leaving it open for the neighbor to find the next morning.

So why go through all the work to replicate the murder of the father on the son, then not go through with raping the daughter like he had the mother? There was a deliberateness to the parallels. He'd even attacked both females in or around the throat.

A shrill scream made Loshak bolt to his feet, heart thundering, his hand fumbling in his jacket for the Glock. His clumsy fingers slipped off the snap, unable to find purchase. Then the noise came again, and he realized it was just his phone ringing. The piercing harshness of the ringtone seemed profane in all that silence.

Heat flooded his face as he shook his jacket back into place. Damn. Jumping at a loud noise like some kind of rookie. He was lucky he hadn't shot himself in the foot trying to pull his weapon out.

At least he was up there alone. Nobody to witness his humiliation but himself. Darger would've teased him, not even realizing she was probably the reason he was going soft.

His phone rang a third time, the sound sending discordant shivers down his spine, before he managed to pull it out of his jacket with shaking hands. His first thought was that it was his hard-headed partner, calling to say she was done thinking it over, that she knew what she wanted, and it wasn't this.

But the number had a Miami area code. Jan? She could be calling him back from a landline.

He thumbed the answer icon. "Loshak."

"Agent, it's Spinks," came the smooth baritone. "Are you in Miami yet?"

The reporter. Loshak shoved aside the combination of disappointment and relief that it wasn't his ex-wife on the other end of the line and shifted his focus back to the case.

"Landed two hours ago," he said.

"Good, because I've got us a lead."

"All right," Loshak said, letting himself out of the children's bedroom. He was happy to take any excuse to leave it behind. "Let's hear it."

"Listen to this," Spinks said. "Six miles away from the most recent crime scene, we've got another house with screens thrown in the bushes and around the yard. Looks like somebody tried to break in and failed. Same method as the Cutler Bay house, right? But that's not even the weirdest part. The exterior of this house is like a twin to the Nicholson house. Same model and shape, same gray vinyl siding, same white trim. There's even wooden steps leading up to a white front door with a brushed brass handle."

Loshak headed downstairs toward the door in question. Brushed brass handle all right.

"When did this happen?" he asked.

"Last night. Looks like our killer tried this house first, couldn't get in, got frustrated and took off for Cutler Bay." Spinks sounded a little out of breath. "Two houses. Six miles apart. One family slept through the night, totally unaware of the creeper prying at their screens, while the other got murdered in their beds. Can you imagine it? The line between life and death comes down to an unlocked window?"

"Well, I'm standing in the Nicholson house right now, so yeah," Loshak said. "I think I can. Where'd you come up with this lead?"

"Friend in the Richmond Heights PD. They talked to a neighbor, but she's not much help. She was on her way home from work when she saw a guy rush out of their yard, hop into a dark sedan, and peel out. No license plate. No make or model."

Loshak shook his head. "It's not much to go on."

"Not by itself, but they also found a pile of cigarette butts where he might've parked and cased the place for a while. Winstons." Spinks didn't even pause before saying, "I know, I know, still not much to go on, but they also got a shoeprint from underneath one of the windows. Should be able to get the size."

Maybe even brand, Loshak thought, his mind going back to the gently handled cabinetry. "Is that it?"

"I mean, taken altogether, that's kind of a big deal, Agent," Spinks said, a hint of sarcasm creeping in. "We're starting to get a picture of this guy."

"It's pretty fuzzy," Loshak said.

For a few seconds, silence passed back and forth through the cell towers.

"Tell you what," Spinks finally said. "Meet me for lunch. My treat. We'll talk about the case, and you'll get a free meal."

The hollow gnawing in Loshak's stomach made up his mind.

"Why not?"

CHAPTER 4

From the outside, the Chuck Wagon looked as if it had been built in a closed-down Cracker Barrel, but most of the vehicles in the parking lot had Florida plates, which Loshak took as a good sign. If the locals liked it, then the food was either good enough to eat or cheap enough not to complain.

There was a decent crowd in the diner, considering it was late afternoon, that in-between lull when it's too late for lunch and too early for anyone under 70 to eat supper. A few tables of seniors were taking advantage of the Gumbo Limbo AARP Special. Everybody had a coffee, except for a kid of about five or six blowing bubbles in a glass of chocolate milk, stirring up the layer of dark brown syrup at the bottom.

Sticky-looking checkered tablecloths draped the tables, and old Coke signs hung on the walls next to art depicting scenes of Wild West nostalgia. It was cozy in that gruff way western-themed places always tried to project. Rustic. A little rugged. Reminded Loshak of his grandfather before he passed, a real man's man even on the downhill slope. He could change a tire or flush a radiator by himself well into his eighties, a sweaty six-pack of Miller High Life perpetually within reach.

Loshak lowered himself into a seat by the window, trying to remember the last time he'd changed a tire himself. He couldn't. How pathetic was that? Pathetic

28

maybe, but not uncommon. Nowadays most people couldn't look under the hood of their car and point out the radiator — that was what mechanics were for — but in his grandfather's day, a man who didn't do his own automotive work wasn't much of a man at all. A hundred thousand years ago, a man who couldn't hunt and kill his own woolly mammoth wasn't much of a man at all. It was strange how these things evolved. A hundred thousand years from now, what would the marks of masculinity be?

Loshak craned his neck to check the parking lot. No new cars. No Spinks. He checked the time on his phone.

The rustle of clothing behind him brought his attention back to the restaurant. A waitress in a black t-shirt with the Chuck Wagon logo was favoring him with an exhausted smile. Her crow's feet made crinkles in the corners of her blue eyeshadow.

"What can I start you off with, handsome?"

Loshak returned the smile. "Well, I wouldn't say no to more flattery."

She tilted her head back a little when she laughed. It was nice. Made her seem sincerely tickled.

"You don't fish for compliments, huh, you just throw out the whole net."

"I'm not too picky. Whatever I can catch I'll take," he said, drumming his fingers on the tabletop. Almost like a sting to let her know the comedy routine was over. "No, I'm waiting for someone, but I'll take a coffee in the meantime."

"Sure thing."

She bustled off to the coffee pots behind the counter and came back with a mug wide enough to qualify as a soup bowl in most diners.

She winked as she set it on the table. "I'll come get your order when your friend shows up. Holler at me if you need anything."

"Thanks," he said, although she was already halfway across the room.

Loshak took a drink from the soup bowl, feeling a little like he should be using both hands, then set it back down beside his phone. Idly, he pushed the Home button, bringing the screen to life. He watched the clock until the minute rolled over, then the display timed out and went dark. Loshak took another drink of coffee.

Across the diner, the waitress gathered plates from the senior citizens' table. She patted one of the older men on the shoulder before reaching over him. Probably just a warning to let the old guy know she was behind him, but there was something so warm about the way she did it. Friendly. Loshak could imagine how the touch would feel. Affectionate. Reassuring.

Before he could think about it, Loshak picked up the phone, thumbed over to Jan's number and hit Call. While it rang, he told himself that it didn't matter since she wouldn't answer anyway.

"Hello?"

Loshak flinched at the sound of her voice.

"Hey, it's me." He sounded normal, almost breezy. His fingers and hands felt like they had a low-level electrical current running through them, a sort of buzzing numbness, but his voice sounded casual, like he called her every day. Like this wasn't a big deal. Like they hadn't been divorced for a few years now. "I'm down in Miami consult—"

"God, Vick, just leave me alone." The line went silent.

Loshak lowered the phone and stared at her name, at the call timer. Seven seconds. That low buzzing numbness had spread to all his limbs.

Well, that was the reaction he'd been expecting, wasn't it? He just hadn't expected it to happen so fast. Seven fucking seconds. Hell, you gave door-to-door vacuum cleaner salesmen better than that.

"Agent Loshak?" a smooth baritone asked.

Loshak looked up, startled. A tall black man, probably in his early forties, wearing a lavender button-up and pleated khakis was offering him a handshake. He had the sort of long, graceful fingers Jan would've called piano player's fingers.

"Jevon Spinks," the man said.

Loshak took his hand automatically and shook, scrambling to throw off the stunned feeling of Jan's rejection.

"Have a seat, Mr. Spinks—"

"You can just call me Spinks. Everybody does."

The reporter folded himself into the seat across the table. When he grinned, his eyes twinkled and a dimple appeared in the center of his chin.

"I've heard every permutation kids could come up with. From Anal Spinkter to Stinky Spinky. Mr. Spinks doesn't sound a lot less ridiculous to me. Maybe even something you'd name a housecat."

In spite of himself, Loshak huffed out a chuckle. "All right, Spinks it is."

The waitress hustled back over and took their order —

a bowl of the gumbo with crackers for Spinks and a burger with jalapeno straws and barbecue sauce for Loshak. Then she brought Spinks a soup bowl of his own and refilled Loshak's.

"So," Spinks said as he tore open a pair of creamers and poured them into his coffee, "Bad news about the case?"

Loshak paused with his cup halfway to his lips. "What?"

"The call you just got." The reporter slipped one of the empty creamer cartons into the other, then tore open a packet of yellow sweetener. After he added that to his coffee, he stuffed the empty packet into the creamer cartons.

"Oh. No." Loshak took a quick drink, then set the soup bowl coffee cup back on the table a little too hard. "No, actually, that was personal. My ex-wife."

"Mm-mm." Spinks shook his head. "No wonder you look like somebody just kicked you in the beanbag."

Loshak was surprised to find a wave of defensive anger rising up in his chest.

"No, Jan's not like that. Not hostile, I mean. She never was. There's just a lot of baggage left over. Distance. Not just from the divorce, but our daughter… She passed a few years ago. Cancer. Neither of us handled it very well." He shrugged. "And now here we are."

Instead of the standard replies Loshak had gotten used to when Shelly came up — things like *Oh, I'm so sorry* and *Wow, that's awful* — Spinks just nodded.

"How can you, though?" he said, stirring his milky coffee slowly. "Handle something like that, I mean. You expect your parents to die before you do. That's natural. In a way we're all waiting for that day, preparing to become adult orphans. There's a collective script for that situation that we can follow. But losing a kid, there's no social mechanism for dealing with that. Nothing to prepare you for it, to help you cope. There's not even a word for it in the English language. The child who survives is an orphan, like I said, but the parent who survives? Well, there's nothing for that."

Loshak opened his mouth to agree, then realized he was settling in for a heart-to-heart with a guy he'd just met in person five minutes ago.

"You must be one hell of a reporter," he said. "With interrogation skills like that, I'd be happy to give you a job in any FBI field office."

Spinks chuckled.

"Pass. Writing's where my fortunes lie, mediocre though they might be." He tapped his spoon on the lip of his cup and set it on his napkin. "No, uh, my son, Davin, he died in a wreck. About eight years ago. So."

All the cliché responses bubbled up from Loshak's gut like indigestion, but he swallowed them. There wasn't anything he could say to fix it, to bring the kid back. He knew that firsthand. So, he didn't say anything.

"This the first time you talked to her since the divorce?" Spinks asked.

Loshak shifted in his seat, thinking back to Jan packing up everything of hers and leaving. He'd made it home from work just in time to watch her climb into the U-Haul. That had been his last chance. There had to have been a correct thing he could've said then to convince her not to go. She'd looked at him like she wanted him to, like he should've known the right words to say. But he'd just stood on their porch and watched her drive away, swallowing once as the truck rounded the corner and disappeared from view.

"Kind of." He tried to recapture that nonchalance from the call as he said, "She wasn't interested in talking. Not to me, anyway."

Spinks nodded. "My advice? Give it a minute. Let it marinate. It can't be easy just hearing from you out of the blue like that, after however long it's been with nothing. You got to figure it stirred up a lot of emotions, just the sound of your voice."

They fell silent as the waitress came back with their orders. After making sure everything looked right to them, she told them to holler if they needed anything, then headed off toward the kitchen.

Loshak lifted the bun of his burger and raked the jalapeno straws away with a fork.

"I guess you're speaking from experience?"

"Somewhat." Spinks crumbled a handful of off-brand Saltines into his gumbo. "My wife and I are still together. Not that it's my doing that kept us that way or your doing that caused your divorce. I just do well with people."

He dusted the crumbs off his hands and into the bowl, then set to rounding up the pieces on the table and sweeping them into his hand.

"It's like being a reporter. You start out with the facts, then work your way up to chasing down the truth. Lot of people think truth and facts are the same thing, but they're not. Facts lack context, lack meaning. They are, period. Truth comes from inside, comes from human desires and the forces we exert on the world to achieve them. Facts are simple, but the truth rarely is. Two guys could, say, steal ten grand from their employer, right? But if one did it to pay for his kid's emergency surgery and another did it to pay for a couple of jet-skis, well… Now we have two stories with the same basic facts and vastly different truths."

"Maybe." Loshak set his fork aside and picked up the burger with both hands.

"Like you can list the biographical facts about somebody in their obituary or a feature, but it wouldn't begin to tell you the most important things about them. There's more to a person than name, age, cause of death, and occupation. All the depth, all that's interesting, exists outside of that list. The stuff in between, the stuff that makes them an individual, the things in life that brought them joy or pain or sorrow. Their passions. Their obsessions. That's where their truth lies."

Spinks paused in his monologue long enough to take a bite of gumbo and swallow it.

"Which is why I think we should go talk to the boyfriend of the second victim," he continued. "The one the cops like for the murder. We find out his truth, and I bet you we poke holes all over their theory."

"You sound pretty sure."

"I am pretty sure." He downed another spoonful of cracker-thickened gumbo. "Now that you're working the case? Let's just say I like our odds."

"Hang on now," Loshak said, setting his burger down and wiping his hands on a napkin. "I'm just here for a couple days. Enough time to give the task force a profile and answer any questions they might have, then I'm headed back to Quantico. I've got classes to teach."

"Yeesh. That sounds awfully boring."

A list of the times his partner had almost died since they started working together ran through Loshak's head. He picked up his fork and stabbed a few jalapeno straws.

"In this line of work, boring means it's all going to plan. It's the exciting stuff that gets you killed."

Spinks set his spoon down and took a sip of coffee. "Yeah, well, while you're here, let's profile the guy the cops think did it. If you're on board with their theory, you can hand that over to them. If you're not, we can tell them why they're barking up the wrong tree."

Before Loshak could agree, Spinks pointed at the pile of jalapeno straws he had scraped off his burger.

"You could've just ordered those on the side, you know."

"I never really cared for jalapenos," Loshak admitted. "But I had a bad case of pancreatitis a while back. No more spicy food for me, the doctors tell me. One of the side effects, I guess. I've never had a problem with it to this point, but I like to test out my digestive tract every now and then. Pop a couple of hot peppers in the works. See if it can still keep up."

"Miami rush hour traffic is where I would test out my digestive tract, too." That chin-dimple appeared again when Spinks laughed. "No, I'm just messing with you. Eat up. I've got leather seats. We'll hose 'em down if your experiment doesn't work out."

CHAPTER 5

As he and Spinks crossed the parking lot of the dumpy apartment complex, Loshak took in the bars on the windows and torn screens. No grass or trees grew anywhere along the building. The landscaping had been torn out at some point — roughly from the looks of it — and all the vacancies had been filled in with rock. Graffiti was scrawled or scratched all over the walls and railings in the stairwell, some of it fresh and blunt, some of it fading away.

Loshak followed Spinks up to the third floor. The door the reporter knocked on had *Candi eats shit* carved into the peeling green paint, jagged letters scrawled under the peephole. A classy touch.

They heard movement inside right away, but the door didn't open immediately. Loshak thought he caught a glimpse of action behind the peephole, a shifting of light and shadow. He gave the peeper a friendly smile and wave.

A deadbolt *thunked*. The door opened a few inches, the chain lock stopping it short.

And now a face hovered in the opening, a guy in his early twenties with wide, scared eyes. The kid was wearing a Hollister t-shirt and American Eagle sandals. Luxury brands Loshak somehow remembered from the times he'd gone to the mall with Shelly way back when. The preppiness looked out of place in this dump.

"Chris Morely?" Loshak asked.

"Yeah, what?" His lips pursed like he was spitting the words out. All defense and aggression, like he wanted to fight.

Loshak knew there wasn't a whole lot of difference between fear and anger with young men. Being afraid brought all of their inadequacies to the surface, exposed the places where their strength and masculinity wasn't enough. It made a lot of kids that age feel like they had something to prove.

But before he could put the kid at ease, Spinks stepped up.

"Easy tiger, it's me, the one who's on your side. This is Special Agent Loshak with the FBI. He's straight out of Quantico, here to get things rolling a little more smoothly with the investigation. Can we come in for a minute and talk?"

"About what?" Chris snapped. "It's just a matter of time until your cop buddies charge me with killing Lacey. They've been following me everywhere, harassing me and shit. Why bother looking for the real killer when they can pin it on me and go stuff their faces at the donut shop?"

Spinks laughed.

"Man, it's no wonder they want to knock in your punkass teeth. Look, Agent Loshak hasn't been biased by their opinions yet. He's just what you need. New blood, fresh eyes. A whole different way of doing things. Dude doesn't even like donuts."

Chris didn't immediately tell them to get lost this time. He sized Loshak up.

"I'm just here to find out the truth," Loshak said. "Although that was a lie about the donuts. I like 'em. Donut holes mainly, but I'll settle for the rings if I have to."

The kid squinted at Loshak as if he couldn't tell whether that was meant to be a joke or not. A few seconds passed, then he closed the door. The chain rattled. The door swung open again, and Chris stepped back to allow them through.

Inside, the little apartment was a trash heap. A leather sectional covered in clothes that reeked of body spray and aftershave; a glass coffee table with pizza boxes, beer bottles, and Xbox controllers scattered across the top; an entertainment center stacked high with video games, DVDs, and more clothes. The huge flat screen even had smudges across its face, the sort you would expect to see from a three-year-old who didn't know better than to touch it yet.

Loshak shoved a pair of wrinkled cargo shorts out of the way and sat down at one end of the sectional while Spinks made himself comfortable in a laid-back gamer chair across the room. Chris perched on the arm at the other end of the couch, glancing back and forth between the reporter and the FBI agent.

"Why do you think the cops are so convinced you did it, Chris?" Loshak asked.

"So I could steal a bunch of expensive shit from her and pawn it," he said, leaning his elbows on his knees awkwardly. "They found out I'm in a lot of debt, so they're saying I did it to pay off my student loans and credit cards. Like I would do that to Lacey over something so fucking petty."

"Is it true that she had a restraining order against you?"

Chris snorted with disgust. "Lacey did that kind of crap. Ask her last three boyfriends. She liked being spent big money on, and when you ran out of cash, she was on to the next guy. Major gold digger. And if you tried to get anything you gave her back — boom — suddenly you're an abusive asshole who used to beat her, and she just barely managed to escape your clutches with her life. Pretty effective way to keep you from getting your shit back if you're not allowed to call her or stand within a hundred yards of her."

"You tried to get her to return something you gave her while you were together?" Loshak asked. "What was it?"

"A Louis Vuitton bag. Getting it's how I maxed out my last card. That's why I'm saying, if I supposedly did all this to steal valuable crap, then I did a piss-poor job."

Loshak and Spinks looked at each other.

"Why's that?"

"I saw the list of stuff they were looking for when they came over to search my apartment," Chris said. "A bunch of cheap-ass jewelry and some shitty electronics? I'd have to be a moron to waste my time on that when her collection would net me ten grand easy."

"Collection?" Loshak asked.

"Of designer handbags. You know, fancy purses. Lacey had a whole closetful. Fendi, Chloe, YSL — you name it. She was a freak for that stuff. We were together, what, eight months? And I ended up buying her three."

Chris shook his head and frowned down at his hands, but the break in his voice gave him away.

"She always needed more. I didn't really get why, but I wanted to give it to her, you know? Delay the inevitable a little while longer. And it was always really nice to see her happy and know I'd caused that, even if it was just until she saw something new."

CHAPTER 6

"Well, what do you think?" Spinks asked as they drove away from Chris Morely's apartment building.

"Motive could be personal. Morely might've killed her for leaving him," Loshak said. "Or because she wouldn't give him the bag back. Or he could've left the bags so he would have a plausible way to cast doubt."

Spinks made a weird hissing noise, and Loshak realized the man was laughing.

"You think that kid could come up with something that complex?" Spinks shot a sidelong glance at him. "The one we just talked to, living in a pig sty, who couldn't even be bothered to return his games and DVDs to their cases or his clothes to his dresser? That one?"

"Yeah, I don't like him for it, but that doesn't mean it's impossible."

Loshak watched the liquor stores and pawn shops blur past. Now and again his eye caught on a shattered window held together with duct tape or a crumbling brick façade.

"The thing about the bags makes sense," Loshak mused. "A random burglar might not realize they're worth anything."

Especially a burglar who stole entire drawers of cheap silverware. It didn't hint at an eye for detail. This was a guy who didn't know luxury from junk. Or at the very least wasn't on the lookout for it.

That plus the seeming randomness of the houses their

murderer had selected, the inconsistencies between victims, the screens strewn across two yards six miles apart — Loshak was getting a strong sense of chaos from this guy.

He squeezed the bridge of his nose, trying to push back a threatening headache. Chaos was an investigative nightmare. They needed predictability if they wanted to catch him. It was damn near impossible to predict what a criminal would do next if they didn't know themselves.

"So, what do we do now?" Spinks asked, an undercurrent of excitement in his voice. "How do we verify that the kid isn't our murderer?"

Loshak lowered his hand and stared out the windshield at the street. They were leaving behind the ghetto neighborhoods, moving from liquor, guns, and pawn to fast food and dollar stores.

"Could you take me to Laccy Monroe's house?" he asked.

"Not only can I take you there," Spinks said, "But I can help you search it."

The tone of this declaration surprised a chuckle out of Loshak.

"What?" Spinks shot him a look.

"That was like one of those ending lines just before a show cuts to commercial. Like you should've whipped off your sunglasses and said, 'Not only can I take you there…But I can help you search it.' Then the music swells and *CSI: Miami* flashes across the screen."

Spinks laughed. "I might have the same fair complexion, but Horatio Cane I ain't. Little too serious for my blood."

"Maybe not," Loshak said. "But you're having the time of your life chasing this case, aren't you?"

"Are you kidding me? Of course I am. Name somebody who wouldn't. Most people spend their whole lives wishing for real-life drama to fall into their laps so they can be the ones to figure it out, to come out the hero and prove that they're worth something besides the nine-to-five."

Loshak shook his head. "Most people who end up in Sherlock Holmes' place aren't running around solving crimes, they're wishing for it all to be over so they can go back to their nice, boring lives. Back to comfort and safety."

"I'm not talking about Maslow's hierarchy of needs here," Spinks said. "But if I were, we'd be getting pretty high up there, closing in on self-actualization and shit. But I'm talking about what people think they want. Entertainment, excitement, intrigue. As a kid, everybody thinks they're cut out to be James Bond, and that never really goes away. It doesn't have anything to do with reality. It's that little thing that makes kids run around with a notebook and magnifying glass and spy on their neighbors in the name of playing detective. The thrill people get when they figure out the killer before the show's CSI team does. If you figure out who did it and why, congratulations, you're smarter than Death and you get to go on living. At least, that's the illusion."

Spinks shifted in his seat, leaning over the steering wheel a little, as if he were really gearing up now.

"And then there's the morbid fascination angle to consider. The voice in your head wondering how close you can get to death. Leaning out over the edge of the void and hanging on with one finger. Some primal part of all of us wants to see blood and guts and know that ours are still tucked safely away inside our skin. If you give the average person two news articles, one about a cat that crosses the country to return to its loving family and one about—"

A computerized tune interrupted the reporter's rant. Spinks leaned back in his seat and dug into the pocket of his khakis.

"…one about the grisly murder of…" His lecture faltered as he checked the screen. "…of a whole family…"

Loshak caught a glimpse of the name *Lisa* over a picture of a mocha-skinned woman with a beauty mark by her eye and her face propped on her fists before Spinks swiped to ignore the call.

"Well, you get the idea." Spinks dropped the phone into the cup holder as if he couldn't wait to get it out of his hand.

Loshak waited, sure there was more. This had the feel of a practiced sermon.

But Spinks just sat back in the driver's seat and leaned his elbow on the door's armrest. Distancing himself from the phone or from Loshak?

"Telemarketer?" Loshak joked.

Spinks gave an unconvincing smile. "Nah, my wife."

Loshak wasn't really sure how to respond to this. He tried a smile, but it felt worse than the one Spinks had just put on. And the silence was stretching out as cars and buildings passed on either side of the car. Getting awkward the longer it went on.

He glanced over at Spinks, accidentally catching the reporter's eye. Instead of looking away and pretending like nothing had happened, he held the contact until it was weird. He almost expected Spinks to chuckle at the awkwardness, but he didn't. Instead, he looked solemn. A little intense.

"Avoiding your wife, eh?" Loshak said, unable to reel in that little smile curling his lip.

"Yeah. I guess so," Spinks said, finally shifting his gaze back to the road. "I mean, she likes to check up on me, which I don't mind too much, but does it always have to be a call? She knows I'm busy. Send a text, you know? I'll text back at my convenience. There's a system in place for this. A standard operating procedure the rest of the world has embraced. She's got to be the only person alive who refuses to text."

Loshak adjusted in his seat, glad to be out from under that steely gaze.

"Not the only one," he said. "I hate texting. Hate typing with my thumbs, I guess. I'm too slow. Then you have to wait for them to get back to you. It's frustrating. I'd rather just call, get an answer, and be done with it."

Spinks nodded, but as if he hadn't really heard. He looked so glum that Loshak felt compelled to say more.

"You should be thankful, you know, that someone cares enough to check on you." He tapped his thumb on his knee. "I think I kind of took that for granted back in my day. Let it get away from me."

"Yeah, no, I mean, I know I should be, and I am plenty thankful to a point," Spinks said. "It's just… it's not how it used to be for me and her, you know? My wife, I mean. Since Davin died, it's more like me and Lisa… well, it's like we're best friends, I guess you could say. We joke around.

Have fun. We talk and eat takeout and watch shows together snuggled up on the couch. But it's not a real husband and wife intimacy, not like it used to be. It's more like we're roommates who sleep in the same bed. The other side of our relationship suffered some kind of wound that won't close, won't get better."

He scratched the back of his neck viciously, then shrugged.

"I've tried everything I could think of to fix it. Tried for years and years. Guess we both did. Like that kid Morely, buying his girlfriend all those designer bags so she would stay with him. We were trying to cling to what we were before, but eventually you've got to face that this is the reality now. Lisa and I care about each other, love each other even, and we still have everything in common we did before, but there's no heat left between us. I mean, I'd never leave her, but it all feels empty in a weird way. Like this big lie we're both perpetuating."

Loshak's mouth fell open, but he covered this with his hand as if he were scratching his lip. It was a hell of a personal revelation to just throw out there. Poured out like Spinks had been waiting for somebody to ask. He cleared his throat.

"Sorry I busted your balls about it, man," Loshak said. "Losing that... It's awful."

He thought about Jan's voice on the phone. *God, Vick, just leave me alone.* Awful wasn't the word for it. It was something worse, something bigger and smaller at the same time. It crawled inside you and chewed and poisoned. But when he tried to put the thought into words, it squirmed away, afraid of the light.

47

"It… sucks."

"Yeah, well, what are you gonna do?" Spinks said, and this time his smile was more genuine. Sad, but real. "Tragedy comes along without warning and rips your life up. Does permanent damage. And sometimes, even when you survive the initial onslaught, you're just not the same after. You can never heal quite right, you know?"

They were quiet for a beat, both staring out at the murky twilight surrounding the car.

"No one is safe in this life. Not from random acts of violence. Not from cancer."

Loshak winced, thinking instantly of Shelly, but Spinks hadn't noticed and kept going.

"Not from heart disease or car accidents, and on, and on. Just look at this case with the missing silverware drawers. Even home in bed at night you're not safe, you know? And it could happen to any of us. Any one of us."

He turned to Loshak now, made eye contact, a sort of haunted look about him.

"You could be next," the reporter said.

He shook his head a little. Smiled.

"Or it could be me."

CHAPTER 7

In sharp contrast to Chris Morely's graffiti-pocked apartment complex, Lacey Monroe's house sat in an upper-middle-class tract neighborhood on a block lined with identically shaped homes. Everything clean. Manicured. Shimmering. Nauseatingly homogenous. Little boxes on endless repeat.

The grass was uniformly short across the neighborhood, every lawn sporting a perfect crew cut, each sidewalk a sprawling white strip of concrete clear of cuttings or dirt.

The siding color varied from house to house — probably the only way the residents could tell which one was theirs. Lacey's was blindingly white with maroon storm shutters that looked as if they'd been painted recently. Even the lock was a new-looking electronic job.

The yellow scrap of police tape across the jamb was the only clue that all was not right in this perfect neighborhood. The telltale sign that death had come ripping.

Loshak made a quick call to the department to get the code for the door, then let himself and Spinks inside. Like the Nicholson house, the place was as silent as an empty church. Stark and eerie.

Just inside the door sat a dark wood hall table. A clear vase full of multicolored glass rocks stood next to a shallow seashell bowl for keys, coins, and other small odds and ends. A stormy seascape hung over the table, a pink flat-billed hat stamped with white Gucci logos dangling from one corner of its gaudy silver frame.

Loshak stared at it. Except for the hat, this looked like a hallway decorated and paid for by a middle-aged man. He flipped open the folder, paging over to Lacey's section.

There it was. Her sugar daddy at time of death was Nate Fischer, a forty-three-year-old from Coral Gables and the contractor who'd built the tract houses on this block as spec properties. Married with three kids. In good standing with the community, if you didn't count the mistress half his age across town. Fischer had been questioned, but nothing had come of it.

Although a wealthy contractor with a mostly stable family life didn't feel right to Loshak, he jotted down a note by Fischer's name anyway.

Check shoes. Smoker?

A contractor would be familiar with the low impact drawer guides like the ones from the Nicholson's silverware drawer. Or he could just be a connection. Maybe the killer had worked on one of Fischer's crews, seen Lacey around the job site visiting and followed her home.

Or maybe Loshak was just grasping at shadows with this drawer thing. Trying to find order in the chaos.

All the same, he added *Crew* to his notes, then flipped the folder shut.

Up ahead, Spinks had stopped at the end of the hallway, one arm crossed over his chest, hand cupping his chin and covering his mouth.

Loshak edged around the reporter.

Shards of glass littered the floor, remnants of the

shattered coffee table stuck to the hardwood by dried blood. Lacey had bled to death just in front of the suede and leather sofa. Her arterial spray dotted the upholstery.

Loshak glanced over at Spinks, who was staring down at the blood smears, almost black against the dark flooring.

"If you need to wait outside—" He cringed at how loud his voice sounded in the silence of the empty house.

"I've seen worse," Spinks said after a second, his voice pitched appropriately low. He shrugged. "Been working the crime beat for a while now. And I spent a couple years in the Pork & Beans when I was a kid — the Liberty Square projects. Plenty of murder scenes right in the open out that way. They usually didn't get around to hosing down the mess from the shootings and stabbings, just let the rain deal with it."

Loshak grunted a noncommittal reply, deciding not to mention the stricken look on Spinks' face. This would be the worst of it, anyway.

He consulted the file. "Bedroom's this way."

They made their way around the edge of the living room and down a short hall. An open door to their left revealed a modern-looking bathroom full of chrome and dark wood surfaces. Directly across the hall was the bedroom.

The beginnings of an orange sunset shined through the windows flanking the bed. The wood-slatted blinds on the right were shut, but the ones on the left had been pulled up halfway. Their bottom hung uneven to the extreme, one cord dragged out much farther than the other. That window was shut now, but according to the report, it had been cracked the night Lacey was murdered. Her killer had pushed it open the rest of the way and climbed inside.

Loshak went to the window and turned his back to the panes, facing the room. Standing where the murderer had stood, seeing what he had seen.

Right next to the hall door was a walk-in closet, its folding doors open wide. Loshak stepped inside, vaguely aware of Spinks shadowing him. Dresses, skirts, and tops hung in a row along one wall. Below them were three shelves' worth of shoes — heels, wedges, sneakers, flats, sandals, all designer brands. Went a long way toward confirming Chris Morely's diagnoses: Lacey had liked the finer things in life.

Behind Loshak, Spinks whistled.

"$1400," the reporter said.

Loshak turned around to find him bent over a shelf full of purses. In one hand, he had the label for a brown one with LVs printed across its sides, in the other, he held his phone.

"It says this one is worth nine hundred used."

Spinks moved on to the next purse and typed something into his phone.

"Seventeen hundred and fifty! I'm in the wrong business. Handbags. That's where the money's at."

And there were at least a dozen on the shelf. That ten-grand estimate wasn't looking far off. Maybe even a little low.

"No way could anybody bent on robbing this place walk right by the money in this closet." Spinks gestured to the shoes. "I'm no expert on women's shoes, but even I know a pair of Manolo Blahniks like that would pay for a decent used car."

"Yeah, the Morely robbery angle isn't looking good."

Loshak backed out of the closet and strode down the hall, taking a right into the open dining room and kitchen area.

The cabinetry here looked high-end, just like everything else in Lacey's house. Bright blonde wood, almost glowing compared to the dark floors. The color of the stain was probably called something like Rustic Hickory or American Honey. Amid all that light, the missing silverware drawer looked like a black hole. The end of one metal guide had been bent over and the other was smashed open, as if someone had frantically ripped at the drawer until it came free.

That might indicate that their murderer had learned how to get a drawer out without damaging the hardware between kills. Or it might indicate that he'd been in a hurry after killing Lacey. Then again, it could mean nothing. One day the killer's feeling frisky, the next day he's feeling careful.

More chaos.

Loshak sighed and headed for the front door.

Spinks' footsteps followed him outside. Loshak stopped about halfway up the front lawn.

"Did you already do all your profiling voodoo?" the reporter asked, coming up beside him. "Read the scene? What do you think the silverware thing says about our killer?"

"Not much yet," Loshak admitted.

He scanned the surrounding properties for an optimal spot to case Lacey Monroe's house. "Maybe a desire to leave a calling card. Something to identify himself. Could be taking them as trophies."

But none of those felt particularly convincing to him. Those were the marks of a plan, of some sort of internal logic and order.

He stroked his chin. "Could be chucking them in the dump and laughing at how the cops'll be scratching their heads over that for a while."

There. In the corner made by that privacy fence and the thick trunk of a live oak. It was an ideal place to wait and watch for the victim to come home. Hidden from the windows of the house by the trunk of the tree and from the neighbors by the fence, but with a perfect view of Lacey's front door.

Loshak jogged across the street.

"Hey, where you going?" The sound of the reporter's loafers echoed off the asphalt.

Spinks caught up to Loshak just as he made it to the spot. In the grass around the roots of the oak was a scattering of cigarette butts. About twenty in all.

Loshak rested his hands on his knees and grabbed a twig from the ground. He used it to poke at one of the nubs until it rolled over, revealing the tiny logo.

"Winstons," he said. "Just like at the Richmond house."

CHAPTER 8

It was full dark before Loshak made it back to his motel. After notifying the local FBI field office and the Pinecrest PD, he and Spinks had waited almost an hour for the crime scene techs to show up. And of course there'd been the requisite pissing contest between the Bureau and the Pinecrest Chief of Police over jurisdiction.

Loshak had done what he could to smooth it over with Chief Johns, finally resorting to the threat of media attention, using Spinks as leverage.

"His editors are letting him run with the serial killer story," Loshak had told the barrel-chested officer. "Do you know how the general population reacts when they read a headline like that? Because I do. They're scared at first. But the longer it goes on, the more the fear turns to anger. They start looking for someone to blame. They want to know why the police haven't caught the guy yet. And if they find out that you held out, wouldn't play nice and share with the other jurisdictions trying to find this guy, they're going to roast you."

Johns had finally agreed to play ball but made sure to keep things as slow as possible by breathing over the crime scene techs' necks and arguing with everything that came out of the FBI liaison's mouth. It was going to be some kind of fun getting the task force up and running with Chief Helpful around.

Loshak flipped on the light in his room, illuminating a

pair of full beds — not the advertised queens he'd paid for — covered in satiny brown and blue comforters and matching pillows intended to project class and luxury. All they really did was highlight the age of the trampled green carpet and nicotine-yellowed plaster of the textured walls.

He toed off his loafers, then removed his jacket and laid it on the bed closest to the door on top of his suitcase. He wanted out of the button-up shirt he'd been wearing since Virginia, too, but he left it on for now. His stomach was growling, demanding he order in something edible asap, and he didn't want to be lounging around in a wife beater when his food showed up.

With a weary groan, he dropped onto the other bed, grabbing the remote and the handful of takeout menus off the nightstand. The hotel classics: pizza, Chinese, and a local sandwich shop. He landed on an Orange Chicken combo with Fried Rice. In all his years with the Bureau, Florida's Chinese had never let him down.

He thought again of Spinks. The reporter had surprised him on the ride over to Monroe's place. He'd seemed so strong, so intense, and maybe he still was both of those things. But tonight, after Spinks had shared the background on his wife, he also seemed fragile.

Something about it didn't feel right. Gave Loshak a knotted tightness in his gut thinking about it.

Here was this hard-nosed crime writer in a rough town, this forceful guy who had spearheaded the silverware murders being investigated as a serial case and somehow elbowed his way into being Loshak's right-hand man in the process. And yet he was also vulnerable, almost broken.

At first blush, part of Loshak felt like Spinks was the

kind of guy who'd be fine almost no matter what, a thick skin, an innate toughness to him. The reporter seemed like one of those people who channeled all of his energy into action, into forging ahead, into exerting his force on the world.

And now another part of Loshak worried about the guy. Writing about these crimes would get under anyone's skin — Loshak knew that from working them himself. And after that, he had to go home to a wounded marriage — not a broken marriage — a wounded one.

Still hurting. Still bleeding.

It didn't seem fair.

After he'd called his order in, Loshak kicked back on the bed, turned the TV on, and started flipping through the channels. Commercials, house restoration, game shows, college football, courtroom dramas, COPS, and adult cartoons flickered across the screen, but he wasn't following any of them. His mind kept coming back to the case. The new cabinets, the stolen silverware, the thousand-dollar purses left untouched. The stab-slash motion of the killer's knife. The indiscernible pattern of victims. One family left alive, another family slaughtered. A twenty-three-year-old girl with a string of boyfriends. An older woman living alone.

Something as small as forgetting to lock a window or wanting a little air circulation in your bedroom at night drawing death to you. Anybody could be next.

Jan's face appeared in his mind. Brows drawn low over her green eyes. Glaring down at the phone. At his name.

Anger stirred in his chest. Not just at her rejection, but at how cleanly it cut off any attempt to protect her. An electronic castration. They'd been together nineteen years. Was he supposed to just shrug off the instinct to take care of her because they'd signed some papers and a court had declared them divorced?

Loshak muted the television and picked up his phone. If Jan didn't want to talk to him, he would leave her a message. Tell her to lock her windows, explain how little stood between her and a gory death. If she was still mad at him about Shelly, if she hated him for how he'd been afterward, that was fine. He could live with that. Had for years now. What he couldn't live with was the possibility of not doing anything and ending up in a world where Jan was dead, too.

"What?" The single word speared his eardrum, sharp with a combination of frustration and anger.

The suddenness of it startled him, jumbling the script of the voicemail he'd been preparing in his head.

Instead of the convincing arguments he had formulated, he blurted out, "Jan, it's me. Don't hang up."

She sighed, but her voice softened slightly. "Do you think I just yell 'What' at everyone who calls? I knew it was you when I answered."

For some reason, hearing that loosened some of the tightness in Loshak's chest.

"I'm working a case in Miami right now," he said, finding a piece of the shattered script. "A serial killer. The murders have all been home invasions, houses where a window or door was left unlocked. That's how he got in each time."

He fumbled for the rest of the speech and came up emptyhanded.

"I was calling to let you know so you could check your locks. To make sure."

Jan laughed, the sound harsh and disbelieving.

"Of course it would take something like this to get you to talk to me," she said. "The whole time she was sick, nothing. All this time she's been gone, zero. Barely a word. Work, though, work gets you to call."

Loshak flinched, the words stabbing at the poorly healed scar tissue in his chest. There was a right thing to say next — an apology for being so lost in his own grief that he left her to drown in hers alone in the months leading up to and after Shelly's death — but it was all chaos inside his head.

"Jesus, Jan, will you just check your windows or are you going to try to get murdered out of spite?" was what came out.

Another sharp laugh. This one cut off as she hung up.

Loshak dropped the phone onto the nightstand and shut his eyes, exhaling.

"That went well," he said to the empty motel room, attempting to satisfy some sarcastic impulse in spite of the fact that no one was there to hear it. Or maybe just to stop the bitter resentment in that laugh from ringing his head.

The anger and accusations had been obvious attempts at protecting herself, attacking so he would be on the defensive. Covering for some hidden vulnerability she didn't want him to see.

Loshak felt the corners of his mouth twist up into a wry half-smile. She hated it when he analyzed her. Usually because he was right.

Well, if her goal was hurting him, she couldn't have

done a better job. Nothing could hurt worse than knowing that Jan wanted to protect herself from him.

He stared up at the textured drop ceiling, eyes following the meandering brown line of old water damage. Frustration chased the hurt around inside his gut, some mixture of angry and sad simmering but not quite able to boil over.

Because she'd been right, too.

He hadn't been there. The more Shelly wasted away, the more he'd buried himself in work. Catch this killer, stop this shooter, find this sicko… And still, he'd never felt as useless as he had then. Holding Shelly's hand, watching her die, sitting there doing nothing when any good father would've been saving his child. He'd been nothing then. Not a man, not a father, not a husband. Just a spectator sitting ringside at his daughter's death. Completely powerless.

A series of thumps on the door shocked Loshak out of his guilt trip, the flare of adrenaline lighting up his heart like defibrillation paddles.

The Chinese.

Loshak hauled himself off the bed and fished out his wallet. As he paid, he made small talk with the delivery guy, not really hearing what either of them said. He closed the door and came back to the bed, taking containers out and spreading them across the foot of the brown and blue comforter. He turned the television back on and selected a station at random from the guide, not caring what was on. It was just for the noise, anyway, the comforting sound of other humans filling the empty room. He ate mechanically, eyes on his orange chicken and fried rice.

He felt at loose ends. Unresolved. Not just with his ex-wife, but the case, too. Maybe Spinks was right. Maybe he should stay on a few more days. Sort things out with Jan and keep digging on the case. It would do him good to work one without Darger. See if he still had it in him.

Yeah, he would do that.

CHAPTER 9

The man in black drove through the night, headlights piercing the gloom, neighborhoods of Miami slipping in and out of focus around him. The city blurred and sharpened over and over.

That chemical bliss still swirled around inside his head like a hurricane, thrashing and spitting and lurching at the walls of his skull. It made him clench his jaw, grit his teeth, and his heart thundered in the background at a frantic pace, pumping out a techno throb of blood that he could feel glugging along in the side of his neck.

But it wasn't as intense as it had been half an hour ago when he shot up the last of the coke. He was still high as fuck, jittery and fidgeting and tingling all over, but this was a different kind of high, tamer in a lot of ways than that initial rush, and minus the metallic screaming he always heard in his head at the peak.

The aluminum train was already on its way out.

For the time being, his buzz was idling at that special place where everything still looked sharp and poetic, cinematic. The lights of Miami rolled around him like a scene from a movie. He could feel the soundtrack in his skin, something predatory and dark. Could feel the audience watching as he brought the Winston to his lips and sucked in a lungful of smoke. It curled out of his nostrils as he exhaled, a fire-breathing beast in the night.

A dragon, he thought. Or a demon.

Then, like it usually happened while he was rolling, the man in black found himself parked and staring at a house. He couldn't remember choosing it, just knew that it was the right place, felt it. Like a jump cut taking him from one part of the script to the next. Boring in-between scenes need not apply.

It was a neat neighborhood. Rich. The kind of place where your lawn matched your sidewalks matched your two-car garage and dog and wife's pubes. Across the street sat a tall brick house with a row of columns out front like some kind of plantation.

Through the gauzy white curtains of a first-floor window, he could see the blue flicker of a television reflected onto a fat guy's face. A woman appeared, leaned over the back of the sectional to say something. The fat guy nodded and waved a hand at her. The woman left. A few minutes later, a teenage girl came in from the opposite direction, looking down at a phone. She tapped the dad on his bald head with one finger, not looking up from her glowing screen.

In the car, he flinched, expecting her to get backhanded at the very least, but in the house the dad just said something to her without looking away from his glowing screen.

A house like that, a family like that in a neighborhood like this, they had to be loaded. There would be so much in there he could pawn, gobs of shit he could sell for coke money. Maybe even enough to get a room at a motel for a night or two. Sleep in a real bed for as long as the cash held out.

With a glance down at his fingers, he realized his

cigarette had burned down to a smoldering stub. He couldn't smell the sharp tang of scorched filter — too many lines of coke up the nose before he started shooting it — but he knew it was there. Could remember the chemical stench of it.

He flicked the butt out the window, then shook a fresh tube out of the pack. The wheel on his stolen plastic lighter turned, sparked, sent up a blue and yellow flame in the darkness. He held it long after the tip of the new cigarette was glowing red, staring at his thumb.

The nail melted where it touched the metal rim of the lighter head, a little negative half-moon, but he couldn't feel it. Couldn't feel almost anything outside of that spiraling vortex in his head.

Inside the house, the lights began to go out. One downstairs, then one on the second floor. Another upstairs. The mom walked past the kitchen window, then that light blinked off, too. Pretty soon the only light left was coming from the dancing blue of the television bouncing off the dad's head.

He shoved the lighter back in his jeans and climbed out of the car, letting the door slam. Who gave a shit if somebody heard? What were they gonna do? Even if that fat fuck on the couch heard, there was nothing he could do to stop him. There was nothing anybody could do.

Then he was outside the living room window — no transitions, no creeping, just a sudden jump cut like he was magically transported there by dark forces, by Satan himself — jammed in between some weird leafy bush and the brick wall, staring at the dad who still hadn't looked away from the tube. It was a basketball game, FSU vs.

Duke, and the dad's head was bobbing like he was about to doze off.

He pulled his knife, then started stalking the perimeter. Checking windows. The mom was nowhere to be found, but the light was still on behind a frosted glass window that was probably a bathroom. The daughter must be upstairs in bed. He made it all the way back around to the dad, whose chin was resting on his chest now.

Good. It was good that they were separated. Different rooms, different parts of the house. He could deal with them one at a time that way. He licked his lips, and his fingers uncurled, then gripped the knife again. So long as he got the drop on the dad — ripped his neck open before the fat guy could scream — it'd be easy.

But through the double pane of glass came a weird, deep-noted honk. The buzzer. Game over. On the sectional, the dad jumped, wide awake now, sitting up and leaning toward the television to catch the final score.

"Son of a bitch," the bald man said, shaking his head. His voice sounded muffled and flat through the glass. "Pissed it away."

The dad jabbed at the remote, kind of stabbing it at the flat screen like that would show those bastards. The blue light disappeared, leaving behind a rectangle of yellow illumination coming through a door on the far wall.

The man in black watched as the bald man stood, stretched, then grabbed a windbreaker off the back of the couch. The old guy turned toward the kitchen.

"Annie," he yelled. "You ready?"

The mom appeared in the other door, her shadow cast by the yellow light.

"I've been ready," she snapped, shrugging on a light pink jacket.

"What, you want me to leave in double overtime?" The dad shook his head again, grumbling, "Might as well have."

Together, they turned and headed for the kitchen.

It wasn't that chilly out tonight, was it? the man in black wondered. Enough for a jacket? Sweat sluiced down from his hairline, from his armpits, but he didn't feel hot or cold. Just a sort of blissful warmth.

It wasn't until the front door creaked open and he heard their voices that he realized they were headed outside. He lurched down behind the bush, his shirt snagging on the brick, scraping the exposed skin of his back. He tucked his thighs to his chest and ducked his head down until his kneecaps were pressed into the hollows of his eyes. Full fetal.

Their shoes gritted on the sidewalk. Car doors opened and shut. The engine rumbled to life.

They were leaving the house. Leaving it for him. An offering.

Bright halogen lights swung across the bushes, piercing the leaves and branches as their black crossover backed out of the driveway. He grimaced and blinked, blinded.

Suddenly, the headlights stopped.

He froze, stopping up the breath in his lungs. They knew. This had all been a trap, an elaborate setup. His grip tightened and released on the handle of the knife, tightened, released, ready to plunge it into a throat and rip out the life. Ready to spray blood everywhere in a violent splash of red.

Then the crossover pulled forward. They didn't even

slow down as they passed the stolen car he'd parked across the street.

The air left his lungs in a whoosh, relief making his shoulders slump and his head sag forward onto his knees again. They didn't know. Their brake lights flashed red at the end of the street, then the crossover turned and disappeared.

Left in the dark once more, he stood up and slipped toward the front door. The knob turned easily in his fingers. And why wouldn't it? He was the demon of the night, the god of death. Every door opened to his touch. And when they didn't, the windows did.

When death came for you, nothing could keep him out.

CHAPTER 10

Another jump cut left the man in black inside the house. He found himself standing on the ceramic tile in the foyer, tucked back in the shadows where the light stretching from deeper in the house couldn't reach. Waiting. Listening. Silent. Motionless.

Hunting.

The air was different in here. Dryer. Warmer, too. He hadn't felt cold outside, but in here, it was baking.

Sweat matted his stringy hair to his temples and soaked his black shirt. Old sweat stains bleached jagged circles around the pits and down the back of his collar, turning the fabric more of a brown than black. Rusty-looking in the half-light. He mopped a hand across his forehead and wiped the wetness onto his black pants. Hot as hell.

He checked over his shoulder to make sure he hadn't shut the door. It was open just a crack. Always better to have that way out ready and waiting, to have an exit strategy. Besides, this place could use some airing out.

He turned back and let his eyes adjust to the darkness. To his left, the foyer opened into the living room. To his right was the doorway into the kitchen. Looked like each room led into another all the way around, double-shotgun style, so you could make a circuit of the house without hitting any dead ends.

Just ahead was a staircase leading to the second floor. To the girl. The sacrifice left behind for him. The little lamb laid out on the altar, waiting for the slaughter.

Waiting for him.

He licked his chapped lips just thinking of her up there, tongue catching on flaps of dried skin – sharp scaly white that protruded from the pink flesh, angular little shards like blades.

But first, work. He headed into the kitchen and started checking the drawers closest to him.

Pot holders. Cookbooks. A whole drawer full of those black plastic soup ladles, all different sizes and shapes. He shook his head. Only rich people would have a whole fucking drawer of ladles.

He moved on to the drawers on the other side of the stove. Bingo. The top one was full of silverware, neatly divided by little wooden compartments.

He jerked the drawer out to carry it all. Silverware was a good score. Some of that shit was as valuable as hell. The real silver. The last couple drawers full he'd gotten were cheap shit, but this stuff looked like the real deal to him. Shimmering, almost glowing in the light coming through the kitchen window.

A jump cut later, he was standing in the master bedroom in front of a full-size mirror. In the darkness, with the moonlight behind him, he was just dark clothes on pale skin. Thin, almost skeletal. A face with pits of shadow where the eyes and mouth should be.

A wraith.

A nocturnal creature.

He left his reflection behind and crossed through the silvery light to the armoire. A pair of jewelry boxes sat on its top, one open. Necklaces spilled over the sides like intestines, and rings lay nestled in its shadowy guts. He scooped them out a fistful at a time and threw them into his silverware drawer. They tinkled and jangled against the forks and spoons.

When the first jewelry box was empty, he peeled the lid off the second. More rings, plus earrings — even a pair he was pretty sure were diamonds.

A giddiness filled his body as he dumped that box into the silverware drawer. The feeling swirled into the high, enhancing the euphoria to an almost unbearable throb of bliss. This wasn't just a good haul; from the looks of it, this was a great one. Just thinking about the glistening white rocks he could buy, all wrapped in their little foil packages and waiting for him, made him half hard. He adjusted his jeans, then picked up his silverware drawer full of coke money.

All that and more. But first, there was one more thing to see.

CHAPTER 11

The girl, Mary, shook herself awake, a single hard jerk of her body that shifted the blankets atop her. Eyelids fluttering open in the blackness.

Something there. A dark presence. An intruder.

Oxygen sucked into her chest. A single big breath, dry and harsh but thankfully quiet.

And fear crawled up the length of her spine. A cold feeling that snaked its way under the blanket, under the sheet. Cut off her breathing like a valve clenching at the back of her throat.

Goose bumps plumped in slow motion, one after another, a creeping tautness of flesh that trekked up her back and dead-ended at the base of her skull.

She knew someone was there. Someone was in the room with her.

She could feel it.

Her eyes darted everywhere. Climbed up the shadowed walls. Flicked over the window where the bars of indigo moonlight slanted in. Lingered on the gaping black rectangle of the doorway.

That was the scariest of them all. The doorway. That chasm. Like a portal to some place of darkness.

She ran the circuit three times, checking every corner from floor to ceiling.

But there was nothing there, of course. Just like all the other times she'd gotten a little spooked at night.

71

She finally took a breath. Rolled onto her side. Waited for her heart to slow so she could get back to sleep. It beat so hard that she could hear the blood swishing its pulse in her ears, squishy little clicks playing a speed metal drum part.

Did it ever go away, this fear of the dark? She hoped so. Felt pretty ridiculous. She was in high school now. Still scared of monsters.

She had a stupid geometry test first thing tomorrow morning. Planes and parabolas and scalene triangles that meant everything for 55 minutes the next morning and could safely be forgotten for the rest of her life after. That teacher was always so salty, too. Mrs. Francis with her puffy hair and chunky glasses, neither of which were of this century.

She tugged at the comforter, pulling it a little higher to cover a naked shoulder. If she was completely covered from chin to toes, the night things couldn't hurt her. That was what she'd always believed as a kid, anyway.

The other rule was that she couldn't open her eyes. As long as her eyes were closed, the things that went bump in the night could only hover over the bed. Then it became a game of resisting the urge to crack an eyelid and peek into the darkness.

A small sound — so faint she wasn't even certain she'd really heard it — sent her heart racing again. She squeezed her eyelids shut.

It was probably only Fizgo. That was the name she'd given the mouse in the walls. At least, she hoped he was a mouse and not a rat.

Two years ago, before Fizgo, there had been a different

mouse in the walls. At first, the tiny scraping of his chewing and pattering of his feet terrified her. She thought someone was tapping at her window, trying to get in her room. When she finally realized it was only a rodent doing rodent-things, she'd relaxed a little.

But the noises still kept her up at night. She'd complained about it to her parents, and her dad put out mouse traps. The poison kind.

The middle-of-the-night mouse sounds stopped, but a few days later, she noticed a terrible stench wafting out from the heat register next to her bed. It got so bad that she shoved a pillow up against the vent to block the smell.

So she hadn't told dad about Fizgo. And it wasn't just about the smell. She didn't like the idea of the little guy being poisoned to death. She'd only given him the name in the first place because it made the nocturnal scraping and scuttling less scary. Instead of hearing a sound and lying in anxiety trying to figure out what it might have been, she could tell herself, "It was just Fizgo." But she found that naming the creature had a secondary effect: she'd grown to like him, kind of.

She drifted now in the empty space between the sleep world and the waking one. Safe and warm and floating.

A floorboard creaked, though, a sound with a heaviness to it that she knew could not be Fizgo. And she knew she shouldn't open her eyes — that the one thing she should not do is open her eyes, but she couldn't resist.

She peeled them open the tiniest crack so the eyelashes still touched.

And he was there. A blackened shape. A silhouette outlined by the faint light coming in from the open doorway. A stretched-out figure that was darker than the rest of the gloom.

Without a sound, he stepped closer to the bed.

CHAPTER 12

In strobes of motion, he saw himself on the stairs in the foyer, then in a hallway with carpeted floors, then in the bedroom. He hesitated just inside the doorway, looking at her bed. It had a canopy, one of those gauzy purple curtain things that hung down on both sides of the headboard and tied to the legs in big stupid bows.

The girl lay asleep at the center, her body swathed in moonlight that lit her in purple tones, one arm thrown over her face, the other tucked under the comforter. Between her legs. He could imagine her masturbating, her back arching and her free hand reaching up over her head to grab for the headboard when she came. That was how she'd fallen asleep.

He glanced around the room for something heavy. There was a lamp on the nightstand, but it looked like a piece of shit that would fall apart as soon as he touched it. The trophies on the dresser might do it. He picked up the one with a tiny golden figure on top running.

Run, run, as fast as you can...

He almost giggled at the snatch of nursery rhyme. Yeah, the running trophy was perfect. Heavy. Solid. The shaft of it fit in his fist perfectly. The base was some kind of gray and white stone, maybe even marble.

He crept back to the girl's bed, watched her chest rise and fall with her breath. Rise. Fall. Rise. He hefted the trophy over his head. Fall.

75

He swung.

The base of the trophy smacked the top of her skull with a dull crack, the corner kind of scraping off the side, ripping hair and skin with it. She gasped, eyes wide and terrified. Gurgled. But she didn't scream or make any other noises.

Good girl.

He could see the wet gush of the blood, the deeper darkness where it pumped into her hair and ran down the side of her broken head, slowly soaking her pillow. She lay still except for that wet flutter. Knocked out, probably.

But how to finish it? The ache in his jeans screamed *Knife.* Nothing made him feel as powerful than shoving his blade into someone's throat and ripping it back out the long way, that perfect stab and slash motion that was all his, all one motion that tore their shit wide the fuck open. All of his aggression, all of his power released in a single stroke.

But the fun was over so fast that way. Less than a minute to go unconscious, with death arriving a quick three or four minutes later.

Strangling, now that took time. Sometimes up to ten minutes.

His cock jerked. *Yes. Strangling.*

He grabbed the lamp off the nightstand, the piece of shit finally good for something, and cut the cord free. Wound it around the girl's neck and cinched it tight. Stared straight into the chasm of gloom where her eyes would be. Then pulled.

His whole body went taut as he choked her. His back arched. Every muscle clenched. Face contorted with effort.

She came to suddenly. Squirmed against him. Bucked. Flopped.

Her fingers picked at the cable cutting off her air like frantic little birds. Unable to get hold of it, she slapped at him, his arms, his thighs.

She wasn't all the way there — he could tell by the weakness in her limbs — but she fought nonetheless. He gritted his teeth and wrenched the cord tighter, arms shaking as the line embedded itself in her skin.

For a second, their eyes met. Hers looked silvery gray in the moonlight, with huge black holes floating in the middle trying to swallow him up.

She saw him, saw his face, looked into the eyes of the creature atop her, and started thrashing harder. Hell had come a-callin', and she knew it.

Goose bumps prickled down his arms and legs, and he blinked. Flinched, maybe. Broke eye contact with her.

And now he yanked the cord harder, muscle tremors quaking his abdomen along with his arms.

He grinned, spit hissing through his teeth as air puffed in and out of his lungs. He could have all of it he wanted. The oxygen belonged to him now. He decided who drank of its sweetness and who suffocated.

Bright lights flared in the window. Halogen. Headlights pulling into the driveway.

Shit. The cord slid out from between his fingers, and he scrambled off the bed, putting as much distance between himself and the girl as fast as he could. He wanted to hide. Curl up in the closet or maybe under the bed. But no, those were obvious places. They always found you there, and then the beating was worse.

He looked at the window, wondering whether there was enough roof outside it to stand on, a gable he could climb up onto and hide until they went away again. But when he took a step toward it, his foot smacked into the silverware drawer he'd set on the floor.

Hold up just a fucking second.

He wasn't small. Not anymore. And he wasn't defenseless. He had a big fucking knife now. He pulled it out, the blade catching the moonlight. Not fucking defenseless at all.

He grabbed the drawer full of treasure off the floor and tucked it under one arm, holding the knife in his other, then crept out of the girl's room and down the stairs.

Outside, he could hear a garage door whirring and car doors slamming.

He grinned and clutched the knife a little tighter. These rich fuckers had no clue what was waiting inside for them.

"What the hell?" the fat guy's voice was coming from the kitchen, just inside the entryway from the garage. "Did you leave the front door open?"

Shit. Fuck. He froze on the bottom step.

"You were the last one out," the woman said.

"I shut it. I know I shut it." The guy's voice was spiraling into anger. "Get behind me, Annie."

"What— Oh, put that down."

"Like hell, somebody's in our fucking house!"

Heavy footsteps thumped into the kitchen, all slow and purposeful. Then the man in black heard it.

CH-CHUNK.

A shotgun.

Nope. Fuck this.

"Whoever the hell you are, if you value your life you'll get the fuck out of Dodge right now!" the fat guy bellowed.

But the man in black was already in motion. He jumped from the bottom step, across the gap of the kitchen doorway, and landed hard by the front door.

Cutlery and jewelry crashed inside the drawer like shattering glass.

Behind him, the woman shrieked, and the fat guy cussed up a storm.

He kicked the door open with his toe and sprinted for the car. Slammed into the side, jamming the drawer up against the window as he fought to jerk open the driver's side door. Finally, it came open with a throaty creak. He dove inside, spilling half the silverware on the asphalt as he went.

A fat blob of windbreaker and shotgun was running down the sidewalk toward the street.

The car fired to life on the first crank of the ignition. He tore the gearshift down, slamming it into drive. The tires screamed, and the car lurched out into the street. Out of the corner of his eye, he caught the dad raising his shotgun.

Instinctively, he scrunched down in the seat, face plastered to the steering wheel.

He felt the BOOM as much as heard it, a sound like a hole torn in time and space, a sound that made his stomach feel hollow and weightless like the first hill on a massive rollercoaster.

And he thought he saw a snort of orange flames flare in the sideview mirror just before a round of birdshot tore it off.

CHAPTER 13

Loshak was just shutting off the shower when he heard his phone ring.

It wouldn't be Jan. Not this early. Or at least that's what he told himself before he could get his hopes up.

He stepped out of the tub onto the white hotel bath mat, wiped himself down frantically with the towel.

It might be Darger. Or it might be the local Feds, calling about the task force meeting later today.

He wrapped the towel around his waist, then hot-footed it into the bedroom. The phone was face-down on the nightstand. He flipped it over to check the caller ID.

Spinks.

Loshak thumbed the little green phone icon, raising it to his still-dripping ear and taking a breath to answer. Before he could say anything, the reporter's excited baritone cut in.

"There's been another attempted murder and robbery." Spinks' voice was almost ecstatic. From the sound of it, Loshak thought he must be having the time of his life following this case.

Then his waterlogged brain caught up with what Spinks had said.

"Attempted?" Loshak repeated.

"Our killer bludgeoned the shit out of a high school girl," Spinks said. "Mary Iverson. He was strangling her when the parents came home and interrupted. He ran off.

She's in a medically induced coma because of the swelling in her brain, but they think she'll make it."

Interesting, Loshak thought. If this was their guy, the girl would be a witness who'd seen him up close and personal. Could be a huge break.

If she made it.

"Bet I know what you're thinking," Spinks said. "Eyeball witness, right?"

"Yeah, if it's him."

Loshak headed back to the bathroom to get another towel. He started drying his hair one-handed while he thought.

"Silverware drawer?" he asked.

"Gone. And they found a pile of Winston butts in the street across the way."

"Damn." Loshak stopped scrubbing at his hair and let his arm fall to his side. "So it really was him."

"Sure looks like it," Spinks said. "You've got the task force meeting this morning, right?"

Loshak swabbed at his free ear with a corner of his towel.

"Nine-thirty sharp," he answered, making a mental note to look up the address of a decent local donut place before he left, somewhere he could stop off at along the way and pick up some goodies for the meeting.

"Give me a holler after. Let me know how it goes," Spinks said.

Loshak was sure it was driving the reporter a little crazy to not have full access to the investigation. Probably felt left out, not being allowed in on the secret squirrel task force meetings. The truth was, he wouldn't be missing much.

This kind of thing was almost always a meet-and-greet to try to get the various departments to stop measuring their dicks and work with one another. There'd be five, maybe ten minutes — tops — of actual useful information distributed. The rest would be a lot of hot air provided by the bureaucrats.

After a solemn promise to keep Spinks in the loop, Loshak ended the call. He tossed the phone on the bed and started to get dressed.

As he buttoned his shirt, his thoughts drifted to Mary Iverson.

Their killer had finally made a mistake.

He'd left a survivor.

CHAPTER 14

The man in black was still driving when the sun came up. His fingers twitched on the steering wheel, and his muscles jumped and shuddered. His jaw clenched so hard it ached.

He dug into his pocket, came up empty without even a piece of foil to lick, then reached up and scratched his hair. His fingers came away all greasy. His teeth were covered in a slimy film that tasted vaguely acidic. A reminder of all the coke he didn't have.

He was too wired to sleep. To slow down. Clips of the night before played on an endless loop in his head.

Bludgeoning.

Strangling.

Her huge pupils locked on his. So scared. Knowing he was death come for her.

And then those headlights twirling over the wall. Flashes of halogen making all the shadows in the room jump around him.

And his power ripped away from him. Replaced by fear. Ball-shriveling, pants-pissing fear.

He slammed his fist into the steering wheel, startling a honk out of the sedan.

He saw himself like last night had been a movie. Cowering like a fucking baby, like he wasn't more than nine years old again. Weak, powerless, terrified. All because of some headlights.

"Fuck!" he yelled, drawing the word out, getting louder

and louder toward the end.

He should've finished her then and there. He'd left a witness. Probably ruined everything.

"If they see your face, you gotta finish 'em." His dad, telling war stories again during one of his almost-sober days. Flipping through a snuff book in his cigarette-burnt recliner. "Otherwise, they got you. They got your face, they got you."

He tried to focus on the images in the snuff mag, tried to call the savage images to mind, find escape in the stimulation, brutality and sex intertwined into something incredible, but he couldn't shake the feeling of that moment of fear. It stuck like a bad taste in his mouth.

Going from powerful to small and scared, falling backward through time to when he was a kid. All those searing memories of pain at the hands of his dad, then uncles and aunts, foster parents, teachers. And even worse shit his kid-brain had probably blocked out, hidden, tucked away in the dark places of his mind to protect him.

He couldn't remember the feel of the injuries — the burns, the bruises, the broken bones — only the terror pumping through his veins, the certainty that he was nothing but a thing that they could hurt whenever they wanted, and nothing he did would stop them. That fear was etched into his psyche, a thousand wounds that would never heal over or go away, a thousand scars that would never be gone.

And he saw the girl again. The frightened girl at the end of his outstretched arms, so close to gone for good. Felt the cord pulling free from his hands. Saw her chest lurch to pull in a breath.

And the memory brought all the pain back, all the old fear, the old hurt, projected onto this new failure. Pressing his nose right in it.

"No," he said, speaking directly to the image of the girl in his head, shaking his head like a dog. "Not again. Never fucking ever. No mercy."

He'd heard on the radio that she may survive, and when he saw her in his head, watched the instant replay of that moment when he let her go, he knew she would.

And maybe he deserved that as punishment, he thought. He'd shown mercy, shown weakness, and now he would be punished appropriately. This was the way of the world.

He closed his eyes. Exhaled and tried to let the bad feelings go, just for a little while.

But they wouldn't go. Not without something to help them along.

He glanced at the passenger seat where the drawer rested under a jacket, and that eased the hurt a little.

Sure, he'd lost some of the goods, spilled them all over the asphalt during his hasty retreat, but he still got enough to score. Soon he could sell it off and get what he needed.

Kill the bad feelings. Kill the fear.

He licked his lips. Imagined the needle pricking his arm. All his worries melting to nothing in a matter of seconds. God, yes, he was ready for that.

Probably couldn't go to the pawn shop today. They paid better, but there was too much heat. No, what with last night's fuckup, he would have to be more careful than ever now.

CHAPTER 15

The task force meeting was scheduled for nine-thirty that morning in the Pinecrest police department, jurisdiction of the first murder and home of the ever-helpful Chief Johns. Sure enough, when Loshak showed up at nine-fifteen, Johns was standing outside the conference room with his arms crossed over his extraordinary gut, scowling at the invaders to his territory.

"Morning, Chief." Loshak lifted the box he'd snagged from the local bakery on his commute. "Donut?"

"I have the diabetes," Johns snapped.

That explained the irritability. Johns' doctor had probably put him on a sugar restriction his wife forced him to follow.

"I got two sugar-free, just in case." Loshak balanced his coffee on the conference room's windowsill and flipped open the lid so he could point them out. "I was going to act like they were regular if nobody said anything. See whether whoever ate them could tell the difference."

Johns chuckled a little.

"Well, goddamn. If you're gonna twist my arm." He picked the cruller drizzled with chocolate-looking icing out and tried a bite. "Not bad. Not bad at all."

A fleck of icing stuck at the very edge of his mustache — a key reason Loshak hadn't worn a 'stache since the early eighties. The greedy things were always grabbing a bite of whatever you were having.

"Can't tell the difference?" Loshak asked.

The chief canted his head to the left. "Now, I don't know if I'd go that far. You're always gonna be able to tell a difference between real sugar and that chemical stuff. But I will say this: It beats the hell out of bran-flakes."

Loshak laughed along with the guy at his joke.

"Want the other before I head in there and throw them to the hungry wolves?" Loshak asked, raising the double-dozen one more time.

Johns' hand twitched toward the box, but he brought it back to his side.

"Nah, better see if your lady friend wants it," he said, jerking his head toward the door. "She looks like the type that doesn't do sugar."

"All right." Loshak closed up the box and headed in.

Representatives from the three jurisdictions were already seated, sipping coffee from an assortment of Styrofoam, gas station, and drive through cups. Four of them were women, but Loshak spotted the "lady friend" Johns had been referring to right away. She wore a smart black pants suit that made her skin look even paler and the backs of her eyelids look a faintly bruised lavender whenever she blinked. Her shiny black hair was pulled back into a severe bun like female officers wore them in the Marines, without a single flyaway. Altogether it highlighted an incredibly lean, almost knife-like physique.

The type that doesn't do sugar, Loshak thought.

She didn't look like a detective. No matter how they dressed, detectives just looked like cops in suits. She looked like a lawyer, which in this setting meant she was a fed. Loshak consulted the Rolodex of names in his head and came up with Agent Alissa Torres, the liaison from the local FBI field office.

"Hey-hey, somebody had a good idea," a detective in a rumpled sports coat said, eyeing the donuts. He smiled, revealing a set of rodent-like teeth. Combined with his prominent ears, he reminded Loshak of a mouse.

Loshak gave the box a flourish, then took it to the opposite side of the room and set it on the folding table next to the coffee maker.

"Have at 'em, folks," he said. "But be warned, that cruller with the crisscross icing is sugar-free."

"We won't hold that against ya." The mousy detective was already hovering over the selection. The star hanging from his neck marked him as Lynn Renaud of the Tamarac PD.

Loshak gave him a grin acknowledging his cleverness, then stepped out of the way to let the rest of the horde descend. He'd already eaten his little baggy of blueberry donut holes in the car on the way over. This way he didn't have to share his private stash with the class.

He found a seat along the wall and sat back to enjoy his coffee and people-watch. Donuts were the great equalizer when it came to task forces. You might not like getting thrown into a room with a bunch of folks you'd been fighting over jurisdiction with, but you damn sure didn't mind a free bit of dough with some icing on top. They were almost sacred in a way. Nobody jostled to the front and nobody broke the cardinal rule of one person, one donut. The rings even got everybody talking to one another while they were up there, discussing which kinds they preferred, approving or good-naturedly deriding each other's choices, and letting their colleagues know where they stood on the sprinkles vs. no sprinkles debate.

In a way that confirmed Chief Johns' suspicions while also contradicting them, Agent Torres didn't choose the sugar-free cruller. Instead, she stayed in her seat, back ramrod straight and legs crossed at the knee. She probably wasn't trying to look disapproving, but it was coming across the same.

When the donut business died down and everybody had returned to their seats with a sugary pastry — some wrapped in napkins, others shedding icing onto fingertips — Chief Johns stepped up to the metal podium, flanked by the chief of police from Miami-Dade. German Najarro, Loshak's memory banks said. The chief from Tamarac, Karen Moretti, leaned against the wall by the door with her arms crossed.

"All right, all right, simmer down." Johns patted the air with one wide hand, the other gripping the podium as if he were a high school principal at an assembly. "First and foremost, the only way we will catch this guy is through interdepartmental cooperation." Somehow, Johns managed to say this as though somebody besides him had been the one holding everything up at the scene the night before. "Anything and everything goes through your chief to me. Agent Torres from the local FBI field office has made up a collective database for us to feed information into. Login instructions are on the first page of the packet Chief Najarro is passing out now."

He waited a moment while the packets made their way throughout the room.

"Oh yeah, and once you're logged in, enable

notifications on your phone. That will help keep you up-to-date whenever we've got something new." Johns flipped open a packet of his own. "Pages two through five are a collection of all the information we currently have on the series of home invasion-murders." Papers shuffled as the detectives around the room leafed through their packets. "Six is a profile of the suspect Special Agent Loshak provided us with. Read it in full on your own time. For now, Agent Loshak, would you give us the particulars?"

Loshak nodded and took to the podium.

"Based on the evidence, we're most likely looking at a male in his early to mid-twenties. Unemployed or quick turnover jobs, chaotic personality, hyperactive, probably with little to no self-care skills — poor hygiene and shabby clothes, that kind of thing. Major, major impulse control problems here, possibly the result of a traumatic head injury in his childhood."

Paper rustled as Loshak flipped through his own notes, picking out the pertinent details.

"He probably frequents prostitutes off and on, and his sexual fantasies are likely of the violent and intense variety. We're talking the extreme end of deviant paraphilic behavior."

"Para-what?"

It was the mousy guy, Detective Renaud.

"Paraphilic," Loshak repeated. "Stuff like exhibitionism, voyeurism, pedophilia, sexual sadism."

Renaud sniffed.

"So you're sayin' he's a sicko."

"Yeah. Sure."

Renaud grinned and said, "Why didn't you say that,

then?"

Loshak swept his jacket back and planted his hands on his hips. It had been a while since he'd briefed a task force on a profile by himself. It felt strange. Usually Darger was there to keep things interesting.

"He'll probably already have a criminal record containing the usual impulse control stuff — assault, shoplifting, drunk and disorderly. Between his impulsive behavior and the predilection for sexual deviance, I'd think a history of indecent exposure very likely. This kind of guy flashes people in public. In the alley. On the bus. He simply cannot resist the urge. It was probably one of the first steps he took down the road he's on now."

Clearing his throat, Loshak continued.

"He's unlikely to have a permanent residence, but he might live with a parent. For the most part, he's a loner who doesn't spend time with either men or women. Probably on the very thin side build-wise, undernourished, gaunt, maybe even emaciated from drug use."

Loshak paced back and forth behind the podium now, hitting his stride, no longer needing to consult his notes.

"In terms of the substance abuse, he'll prefer stimulants rather than depressants. Dealing is probably out, but he might've been picked up for possession more than once." Shaking his head, he added, "Honestly, I'd be surprised if this guy wasn't escalating his crimes to feed a serious addiction. The robberies look like his primary motivation, looking for stuff to sell so he can score, though he seems to be developing a taste for the violence."

He paused for a moment, jabbing a finger in the podium.

"We're talking about a chaotic individual growing more frantic, growing even more aggressive and violent. More dangerous and unpredictable. Looking forward, these kinds of cases almost always develop the same way. The longer he goes unstopped, the more he'll escalate."

Loshak left all the implications of that thought to sink in and returned to his seat.

Johns took his place at the podium, thanked him, then opened the discussion up to the floor.

Detective Renaud chimed in first. "We can get together a list of items stolen from the last scene and send 'em out to all the local pawnshops. Guy's looking for drug money, he'll have to come through one of them selling, and if he's jonesing bad enough, he's not going to wait for the heat to die down. He might come through in the next couple days."

"That's good," Johns said, nodding. "Let's get a list of the valuables taken from the Iverson residence made up—"

"We've got one," Chief Moretti said. She glanced over at Agent Torres. "We'll get it in the database asap."

Torres nodded, once. Affirmative.

"All right," Johns said. "Rivera, Calvin, Tal, you guys are on pawnshop duty for the Pinecrest area. Chiefs, I leave it to you to choose the pawnshop canvassing teams for your jurisdictions. Make sure you pass out the lists of items to be on the lookout for and have them especially watching for anybody trying to sell a drawerful of silverware."

Johns scrubbed his big hands together as if he were trying to warm them up.

"Now, who was it talking about the tipster?"

"Right here." A heavyset detective near the back raised

her hand.

"Detective Hwang, correct?"

The detective nodded. "Tamarac got a call two days ago about a creep at a bus station a mile and a half from the Rodriguez murder. Apparently, the guy was bragging about how he'd killed someone. It's possible he was just trying to scare the tipster's son, but the kid seemed pretty convinced it was for real. We've got a follow-up interview scheduled for tomorrow."

"Agent Loshak—" Johns pointed at him. "—would you be all right sitting in on the follow-up with our tipster? See if you can get a read on the guy based on their story?"

"Sure thing," Loshak said. He was going to be in Miami anyway.

"Great. The rest of you see your chief for your assignment. And login to the database before you leave this room, make sure there are no technical issues." Johns probably didn't notice the slight narrowing of Agent Torres' eyes when he implied her system might have flaws. "Let's get this guy off the streets, people."

Dismissed, about half of the detectives stayed in their seats, figuring out the database. The rest shuffled up to their respective chiefs or checked out the remainders in the donut box.

As Loshak excused himself, he couldn't help but notice how quiet the meeting had been without his partner. The whole thing had gone off downright smoothly. He felt the ghost of a smirk touch his face at the thought. That didn't necessarily mean that Darger caused trouble wherever she went. One time didn't prove anything. But she didn't go out of her way to avoid trouble, either. Especially if she felt like the locals had started it.

He checked his watch as he stepped out into the bright sunlight. Just after ten. It was as good a time for his next stop as any.

CHAPTER 16

Jan's duplex was a long, squat house with terra cotta roofing tiles, tan almost adobe-like walls, and brick accents. A row of short, square bushes lined the perimeter of the house. A carport hung off the eastern end, probably an afterthought from sometime in the eighties or nineties, with a little Escape the color of a powdery blue sky parked inside.

Loshak sat across the street in his rental car. He'd finally got one this morning. He wasn't some damn twenty-year-old who wanted to ride around with strangers he met via a glorified hitchhiking app. And he hadn't wanted to ask Spinks to drive him. Not here.

He slid the keys out of the ignition and bounced them in his hand. He was here. She was here. Now what? Just go ring her doorbell and ask her why she was being so hostile toward him? Why did he even care? They were divorced. Wasn't she entitled to hate him now? Wasn't that basically what divorce papers said? When you boiled them down to their simplest intent, weren't they just a license to hate somebody you used to love?

But Jan had never been the hateful type. Not to him. He'd never heard the level of venom in her voice that he'd heard the night before, not even at the worst of their final days together. It hurt him, cut his insides like swallowing shattered glass. Somehow, after everything else, this was what hurt.

For a second, Loshak considered starting the car back up and driving away. But he needed to make peace with her if it was at all possible. To smooth things out so they could both move on.

He got out and shoved the keys in his pants pocket before he could change his mind.

The asphalt on the street turned into sidewalk way too fast, then he was about to step up onto her porch. His foot was in the air, his hand coming up, reaching for the doorbell.

Then he saw the rat.

Adrenaline flared up from his gut and he flinched away, a knee-jerk reaction he'd always had to rodents. Loshak hated the little fuckers, and here was one perched on her front porch like it owned the place.

Except there was something wrong with this one. As the initial shock wore off, he realized it wasn't sitting, but lying on its side, and its fur was matted and stuck down in places. And there was a wet smear on the brick under it. Blood?

Was it dead?

To test out his hypothesis, Loshak cautiously raised his foot and brought it closer to the rat. When the thing didn't move, he kicked it sideways off the porch. It landed behind the bushes with a dull *plop*.

Loshak swallowed hard and tried to suppress the involuntary shiver of disgust. He was a grown-ass man. He knew base psychological fears, the ones your mind stored deep in the hindbrain, were almost impossible to circumvent when you brushed up against them in real life. But he still felt like a pussy for being scared of a dead rat.

That was the sort of thing children and housewives from the fifties were afraid of.

The clunk of a deadbolt snapped Loshak out of his self-loathing. He stood up straighter, his heart thundering in his chest, as the door opened.

Jan.

Her blonde hair was pulled back in a ponytail, and she wore a pair of faded jeans and a pale gray t-shirt that made her green eyes look almost gray.

Loshak braced himself for her to tell him to fuck off.

But her face broke into a smile instead.

"Vick?" She swung the door open wide and stepped out onto the porch, wrapping her arms around him. "What are you doing here?"

Not really thinking, Loshak fell instinctively into the familiar pattern of hugging her — this arm goes here, that arm goes there, rest this cheek against that cheek. The strangest thing about it was how normal it felt. They hadn't touched in years, but it all came rushing back as natural as breathing.

She still fit perfectly in his arms. He could smell her hair — the same Pantene Pro-V shampoo-conditioner combo she'd used since they got married — and under that, her skin. She smelled like home. Not like his empty house smelled now, but the way it used to smell, when Shelly was alive and well, and they were happy, and everything was good.

After a few seconds, Loshak realized he was creeping it up. Jan had asked him a question. He should say something, answer her, but the only words that came to mind were "I was just in the neighborhood…" Obvious bullshit. He didn't want to lie to her, but "I came here to ask you what the hell your problem was" didn't seem like it would go down well, either. She was acting like those two phone calls had never happened, and he didn't want to ruin this warmth.

A series of sharp yips from the doorway saved him from having to answer. One of those ridiculous little purse dogs — a Yorkie, Loshak thought this kind was called — was bouncing around behind Jan, barking.

"Oh, hush, Roxie." Jan stepped back and looked up into Loshak's eyes, the smile still lighting up her face, though now it was tinged with a hint of embarrassment. "Yappy little thing, isn't she? Don't take offense. She's just suspicious of men. You should come inside. The front step's—"

"No place for family reunions," Loshak finished for her. Then he ducked his head and laughed self-consciously.

But her smile just widened. "Come on."

Jan led him into the duplex, through a short hall, then stepped down into a carpeted living room. Loshak followed, avoiding stepping on the yapping Roxie, who kept circling around him.

"Ugh, I know she's annoying," Jan said, bending down to scoop the little dog up. This finally stopped the barking. She cuddled Roxie in her arms and rolled her eyes. "You'd love her at four in the morning. But she's sweet otherwise. And she keeps me company since… you know."

Loshak nodded and sat down on the overstuffed sofa. "Is she the one leaving presents for you on the porch?"

"What?" Jan cocked her head.

"Dead rats?"

Her warm smile evaporated.

"Another one?" The corner of her lips turned down and Loshak saw a flash of Jan's teeth. "Damn him."

"Damn who?" Loshak sat forward. "Is someone bothering you?"

"Never mind. It's nothing."

"Doesn't sound like nothing."

Jan shook her head and took a quick breath in, exhaling loudly.

"It's my landlord. He…" She shrugged as if she couldn't find the words to explain.

Loshak could. "He leaves dead rats on your front porch."

"Yeah," Jan said, scratching the scruff of Roxie's neck absently. "Well, I guess it's a long story."

"Let's hear it," he said.

Jan was quiet for several seconds, staring down into the middle distance. Just when Loshak was starting to think she would finally tell him the time had come to fuck off and leave her alone, she started talking.

"I signed a 5-year lease with the original landlord — I'd lived here a few years already, and she was happy to keep a long-term tenant. Avoid the turnover costs."

"Makes sense," Loshak said.

"Well, a year into the new lease, she died — my old landlord, I mean. Her son inherited the property, and…" Again that shrug.

But Loshak could fill in the blanks for himself.

"He wants to raise the rent, right? And he needs you out to do it."

Jan nodded. "He offered to buy me out."

"But when you said no, he decided to go a different route." He hadn't meant for that to come out so angry, but he was almost all the way through it before he realized he was practically growling the words.

It was as if the sound of his frustration broke open the floodgates for Jan.

"He lets himself in when I'm not home," she said, eyebrows scrunching together. "Moves my furniture around, eats food out of my fridge. Stupid things like that. I guess to screw with me. Once, he took a big bite of a block of cheddar and left his teeth imprints in it. It's too bad he didn't choke on it." She gave a quick shake of her head. "Anyway, when I filed a complaint about it, he lost it. Screamed in my face until this vein on his forehead stood out like a caterpillar. And that's when the rodents started turning up."

Loshak scratched his jaw. "Maybe I'll have a little talk with this guy."

Jan's eyes went wide.

"What?" He was careful to keep his voice neutral this time. "It won't be a big deal. I'll flash my badge, glare a little bit, and that'll be the end of it."

"I just don't want things to get worse somehow," she said, something akin to exhaustion creeping into her voice. "I regret it. Reporting him, you know? I should've left well enough alone."

When this guy was harassing her in the duplex she paid for, messing with her shit, and screaming in her face. Sure, let's just all let woman-bullying assholes do whatever they want! Rage boiled in the pit of Loshak's stomach, but he pasted an unconcerned smile on his face.

"Don't worry," he told her. "It really won't be a big deal. I'll take care of it."

Jan raised an eyebrow. "Like you took care of that mean girl?"

Loshak was so caught off guard by the one-eighty the conversation had taken that he snorted. A little spray of wetness came out of his right nostril, and he hurried up to put his hand over his nose. But he couldn't stop laughing now, imagining that little brat who'd mercilessly teased his daughter, called her a fat ugly cow over and over, staring wide-eyed and terrified at his badge and gun.

"Hey, it worked, didn't it?" he said.

Jan was shaking her head, but the smile was tugging at her lips again. "You were such an overprotective helicopter dad."

"I was not!"

"Moira was an eight-year-old."

"Yeah, but she bitched at a seventh-grade level, if not eighth."

"Oh God!" There were tears standing out in Jan's eyes, but because she was laughing so hard. "I forgot you used to say that. You wouldn't drop it for, like, three years."

She waved her free hand at her face as if all the laughter was making her overheat. "It's probably a miracle you were never arrested. Nowadays, somebody would sue you for scarring their kid for life."

"Says the woman who would scream and throw things at gymnastics competitions if the judges didn't give her daughter perfect six-point-ohs."

"That is not funny." Jan stabbed a finger at his face, getting all animated just like she had ten years before. "I didn't throw anything. You know she had a perfect floor routine, and they marked her down so that Halligan girl could win the overall."

Loshak grinned, the image of his daughter, nine years old and somersaulting across the blue mat in her little sequined green leotard playing in his mind like a movie.

"Do you remember the eyeshadow?" he asked.

The night before the competition, Shelly had insisted that she needed glittery green eyeshadow to go with the leotard. She couldn't win without it, she'd said. He'd been off work that night, and the three of them had driven around to a hundred different stores until they found an eyeshadow that fit the bill.

"Ah, that stuff got everywhere," Jan said, shifting effortlessly from anger to excitement. "It was like every time I washed clothes, it multiplied."

"How do you think I felt, teaching classes and talking to detectives with green glitter all over my suits?"

"And you did that interview with the reporter who wouldn't stop looking at it."

"I'm pretty sure she thought I'd been pregaming it with a hooker."

That memory led naturally to the time in junior high quiz bowl when Shelly had misheard a question — thinking the moderator had asked them to spell the title of a worker who sold sex and bonds — and buzzed in with "W-H-O-R-E."

"That poor kid's face was so red."

"I still say she was basically right. They should've gotten the points."

He and Jan talked about Shelly in the concert choir,

Shelly's all-night-slasher-movie-marathon sleepovers, how many retainers Shelly had lost, Shelly's potty training sticker chart, and first bike, and the stuffed kangaroo she'd dragged everywhere until it had lost both eyes and she'd pulled most of the stuffing out the hole in its side. But neither one of them said her name.

Then they were down to the last memories before the diagnoses.

"And that whole month, she kept emailing you Craigslist ads, remember?" Jan was still smiling, but her voice was quieter now. "'It says reliable right in the title, Dad.' 'They just replaced all four tires.' 'Look at this one, Dad, it gets thirty miles per gallon.'"

That was when the pain hit. Loshak had to look down at his hands because his vision was blurring over. He nodded, not saying that if they'd known back then he would've bought her the goddamn car for her birthday. He ran a shaky hand through his hair and swallowed, trying not to see the skeleton in the hospital bed, stoned on pain medication, all hollow cheeks and papery skin where there used to be endless energy and glittery green eyeshadow.

The living room stayed quiet for a long time. Jan sniffed, a quick sound, as if she didn't want to do it, but she didn't have a choice.

Loshak wanted to tell her he was sorry for how he'd been after. How he hadn't known how to express all the emotions rolling around in his skull. How he'd let work become the outlet for all his anger and grief, and how he'd just kept shoveling more of it in, trying to fill up the empty hole where their daughter should've been. Where his wife should've been.

He opened his mouth. He tried. But the words stuck in his throat and wouldn't quite come out.

CHAPTER 17

The comedown was fucking awful. Always. Every part of the man in black hurt. Face. Chest. Every strand of muscle fiber. It even hurt inside his bones. The marrow ached, a dull throb like an infected tooth.

His scalp felt dry and itchy, but scratching it only made it hurt worse. His hair was greasy. The oil slathered his fingertips when he scratched and smeared all over the palm of his hand, then onto the handle as he opened the door to the bar.

Music swelled around him here, pulsating drums and bass that turned to weapons and beat on his head from every side. He stumbled a little. Secured his grip on the little paper bag in his hand. Resisted the urge to smash both palms into his ears, as much to keep his quivering brain contents in as to block the sound out, or so it felt.

He looked around the bar. Exposed brick everywhere. Peeling paint on the ceiling. Hardly anybody in this fucking cornhole, but they had the noise turned all the way up like it was party central. They wanted it to seem that way so he would feel comfortable enough to slip up, to let his guard down, but he wouldn't.

He never did.

He caught sight of Dmitri at the last booth on the right side, back there where the light almost didn't reach. In the shadows where the marginalized lurk, where the predators prey, where the sweet rocks of life were hiding, waiting for him.

He looked over his shoulder, making sure they weren't watching him, then slid into the booth. He didn't look into the pusher's eyes. Didn't speak. He and Dmitri had done this so many times that it was natural now. There was an ebb and flow to it, almost a partnership, almost a little routine they'd worked out like those ridiculous synchronized swimmers or ice dancers or something.

But the deal wasn't ridiculous. It was sacred. Hallowed. Righteous and pure. The deal was almost as much a part of the ritual as his actual ritual. It filled his body with lightness. Clarity. Holy feelings.

The foil package entered his hand by way of a handshake, his dollar bills leaving at the same time. A trade. A good trade. Nothing anybody could've seen, not even if they had cameras in the dirty, spiraling trim boards along the wall, right in those little pinhead nails.

A prickle of electric excitement raised the hair on his arms, made him shiver. So close now.

He slid back out of the booth and headed for the bathroom, chewing on the inside of his cheek. So close, so close, so close. He tossed his head a little, the strings of his hair slapping against his cheek. Almost there.

He shouldered the bathroom door open with a bang. Turned his face away from the two mirrors on the wall over the "sinks." Lurched into the last stall, the handicrapper, slammed the door shut. The metallic scrape and click when he turned the lock had him hard again, even made his mouth water. His brain recognized it as the sound that came just before the ritual. The announcement that he was on his way to ecstasy.

Once in the stall, he took the lid off the toilet tank and sat it across the seat like a bridge. Then he pulled his kit out of the paper bag. The crinkle of the paper almost made his teeth numb. He scratched his face with jittering hands, oil building up under his fingernails. So close, so close. Time to savor it.

The aluminum can came out first — a Mountain Dew can cut in half — then the needle, then the strip of rubber tubing. The pack of cigarettes slid out of his pocket, and he tore off a filter. He picked at the paper with a filthy thumbnail until it came loose and he could rip a bit of the cottony part off, rolling it up like a tiny sheep. He arranged all his tools on the lid of the toilet tank just right, then started to unwrap the crinkling foil. Set a glistening rock in the can. Licked his lips. Added another.

He picked up the syringe almost delicately, like a surgeon, and stuck its needle into the back of the toilet. You couldn't trust whatever those so-called "sinks" out there were spewing, but water from the toilet tank was safe. They never messed with toilets.

With the syringe, he sucked up a little of the safe water, then squirted it slowly onto the rocks, watching as they started to break down. He used the plunger end to crush what wasn't dissolving fast enough and swirl it around, helping it along. Then he dropped the tiny filter sheep into the mixture. It fattened up, drinking his coke up for him.

"Okay, go time, go time," he mumbled, jabbing the needle into the sheep. When it was all transferred into the syringe, he flipped the needle upright, flicking at it to disperse any bubbles.

Depressing the plunger with his thumb, he pushed the

air out. He did this slowly. Gently. One time, he'd sneezed at the exact moment he was getting the air out of the syringe, and he'd shot the whole load of coke onto the grimy floor of an Arby's bathroom. Fucking stupid shit. Had to get down on his hands and knees to lick it up, but it wasn't the same.

He wouldn't make that mistake again. No. No way.

The rubber tubing snapped and squeaked as he tied off his arm.

He couldn't stop blinking. He was so close. The anticipation was unbearable. Overwhelming. Staggering. He felt like slamming his head against the wall until it bled or running around and screaming at the top of his lungs.

Breath heaved in and out of him now. Made wet sucking sounds on the way in. Shot flecks of spit from between his teeth on the way out.

He could barely tell where his veins were, they were all flat and thin right then from dehydration or adrenaline or something. So after he slid the needle in, he pulled back a little on the plunger to make sure he hadn't missed. A beautiful, bloody cloud swirled in the coke. He exhaled hard through his nose as he pressed the plunger down.

When it hit, that metallic screaming whistled through his head, and all the tension disappeared. *Mama, it's a magic train*, he thought, grinning. The aching in his bone marrow was gone, forgotten. He couldn't feel anything but bliss and warmth and boundless energy. His hands were moving steadily now, smooth.

He packed up his kit and stuck it in his back pocket. Kicked the fucking stall door open. Shot the mirrors on the wall his all-tooth grin.

What were they gonna do, come get him? Not to-fucking-night they weren't. They couldn't prove anything, and even if they did, they could never take him. You couldn't catch a beast, a demon. Their rules, their laws, they meant nothing to him, held no power over him.

He headed back out into the bar, not walking but levitating. Gliding forward through nothing but thoughts.

"Give me a beer, barkeep," he said, sitting down just above one of the red barstools.

Then the beer was there in his hand, cold and foamy. He tipped it back. Crisp and refreshing.

He remembered his dad cracking open tall-boys of Miller Genuine Draft in the summer, the smell of fresh cut grass wafting into the kitchen. The old man always drank deeply on that first one, the lump in his throat glugging and his lips smacking and sucking on the aluminum tube. He said that there was no beer more enjoyable than the one you chugged immediately after mowing the lawn. Never more delicious, he said. Never more quenching.

But the old man was wrong. He'd clearly never shot liquid cocaine into the crook of his elbow, or he'd have been singing a different song entirely.

The man in black finished his mug, lacy foam still clinging to the sides like white ivy. Raised his hand to get the bartender's attention.

Because this beer he'd finished? Well, it was just the first of many. Many, many.

He was buzzing now, his whole body vibrating with the music, perfectly on-key.

That was the great thing about coke. You could drink all night without getting sloppy, without losing your motor skills and slurring and all that shit. The upper and the down balanced each other out and gave you the best of both worlds. Not to mention all the energy coke gave you, helped you get way the fuck up there, way out past Jupiter where there was nothing but important scenes, no inane transitions from place to place. The beer helped you relax and enjoy the ride, gave your surroundings a nice glow. The party would stretch out for as long as the chemicals stayed plentiful.

He pictured the little foil snuggled up against his hip in his pocket. Wanted to reach back and touch it, to assure himself they were still there. Those precious white rocks within.

He'd snort the rest. Make it last. Shooting it was a better high, but it went too fast. He had to ration it. Not like last time. This time he'd make it feel like forever. Because this night was going to be a long one.

It was still early afternoon. Almost nobody there, but the after-work rush would hit soon. As the night wore on, the party would only grow. Become an epic Hollywood flick, with him taking trips to the stall as needed to replenish. He'd feel fucking great for as long as he could and own this place until he was done with it.

This was the only time he felt social. Coked up and drunk. He liked being around the swarming masses of people. Watching them. Part of them. Charming them. Not quite with them, but among them. Like a wolf blending into a pack of lapdogs. He could rip out their throats whenever he wanted, but none of them knew that because he looked just like them.

None of them realized he was the king of their world.

Not while he was out here, laughing and drinking and making merry with the people.

CHAPTER 18

When Loshak and Jan parted ways, she hugged him again. It was a more sober hug, solemn and dignified in place of their joyous embrace in the doorway, but it lasted longer. As if they were both trying to send some strength through the contact, transmit faith and hope through the clenching of the muscles in their hands and arms and torsos to help the other person keep going, even though they both knew it was a lost cause. They could keep going forever, squeezing each other as hard as they could, and she'd still be dead.

"Make sure you lock your doors and windows," Loshak said, almost tripping over Roxie as he stepped out of the embrace. "All of them. Double check."

Jan didn't look happy — whether because he'd come back around to talking about work or because he was telling her what to do, he didn't know — but finally she nodded.

"Be careful out there, Vick."

He smiled. "I always am."

He started down the sidewalk, turning back when he got to the street to wave at her with his keys in hand. She returned it with a much smaller gesture, still frowning, then disappeared into the house with Roxie trotting at her heels.

Loshak kept up the charade until he started up the rental and pulled away. He rolled around the corner and parked a few houses down, then doubled back on foot through the backyards to Jan's building.

Her landlord, he'd learned from his ex-wife, lived in the other side of the duplex. This asshole was letting himself into Jan's house? Well, Loshak would return the favor.

From the cover of an overgrown oleander, Loshak cased the landlord's side of the duplex, searching for the best way inside. His gaze fell on the sliding glass door that led onto a second-story deck.

There were things Loshak knew from his years in law enforcement, and one of them was that sliders generally had shitty locks. Not only that, but most people didn't bother to lock them at all when they weren't accessible from the ground floor. It was a favorite entry-point for burglars. He reached up, hands gripping the wooden banister over his head, and lifted his feet the first few inches off the ground. Almost instantly, his arms started shaking so bad he thought he wouldn't make it. Good lord. Could he really not do a single pull up anymore?

About halfway up, his progress stopped, arms seizing up at just less than a 90-degree angle. Locked tight. He gritted his teeth, pushed harder. Involuntary grunts emanated from deep within his throat, but his biceps were dead. Shaking like a pair of maracas was about the best they could muster.

And now the pain was spreading into his core, abdominals and shoulders starting to quiver with the strain as well.

Shit.

He wasn't quite high enough to bend at the waist and rest his top half on the wood, to shift his weight off of his useless triceps and deltoids. He kicked out wildly with his feet, trying to propel himself upward. His toe caught against a diagonal support beam.

Yes. Leverage.

He pushed himself the last little bit until, at last, he could swing a knee onto the deck floor.

He crawled over the rail and onto the deck and stayed on hands and knees for more than a full minute, breathing heavily, tremors still rattling his arms and chest and back, pricking him with pins and needles.

God, he was getting old. Why was he doing that?

When at last he rose and walked the length of the wood planks, he found the sliding glass door unlocked, as he'd figured it would be, and let himself in.

Nobody was home.

The place was decorated in old lady traveler chic, full of knickknacks and doilies and souvenirs from various attractions around the US. Even the fridge was covered in an impressive collection of magnets. Some from different states, some depicting kittens and cats wearing fancy old-fashioned hats, even a handful of neon-colored alphabet magnets. Given the assortment of the decor, Loshak thought it was likely the psycho landlord hadn't gotten around to moving all his mom's stuff out yet. And judging by the takeout boxes and half-drunk Big Gulps displayed on the coffee table, he probably wasn't in any big hurry.

Loshak checked his watch, then grabbed a floral-print kitchen chair and pulled it up to the fridge to play with the magnets.

Half an hour passed before a car door slammed in the driveway.

Loshak moved his chair, repositioning it in front of the door, then pulled out his badge and held it up, ready and waiting to startle the fucker.

The front door swung open, admitting a portly, tanned guy in his late twenties or early thirties. Dan Seidel, according to Jan.

"FBI," Loshak said, wiggling his badge.

Dan jumped, his eyes bugging out. Then suddenly, his hand was going for his back.

Loshak was on his feet in a second, gun in hand. "Drop it!"

"Whoa, whoa, whoa!" Dan yelped. "Don't shoot! I surrender!" Very slowly, he pulled the gun from his waistband, holding the barrel pinched between his thumb and forefinger like a dirty diaper or dead fish. He offered the piece to Loshak. "I'm giving it to you, see?"

"Set it on the ground," Loshak snapped.

"Yeah, sure, that's what I was going to do," Seidel said.

Still moving at a glacier's pace, he bent and placed the gun on the foyer floor, then stood again with his hands raised.

The hem of his faded red t-shirt crept up to reveal a sliver of sun-browned flesh. The shirt said *Señor Frog's* across the chest and was at least two sizes too small. Loshak figured it probably didn't matter that the shirt didn't fit. Dan Seidel struck him as the type of guy that went shirtless most of the time, whether his physique warranted it or not.

"I assume you have a concealed weapon permit?" Loshak asked.

Seidel nodded. "Yeah. Definitely."

They stood there for a second. Neither one said

115

anything.

Then Seidel looked down at his gun. "Should I, like, kick it over to you?"

Loshak couldn't help but laugh. The air came out of him in a huge puff, ninety-nine percent relief.

"That won't be necessary. Stay there a sec." He marched over to Seidel and picked up the pistol, then spun the barrel and let the brass drop out into his palm. The bullets clattered as he dropped them on the counter. The empty revolver went on top of the fridge.

"All right." He snagged his dropped badge off the floor by the chair and stuck it back in his sports jacket. "Why don't we sit down, Dan?"

"Why?" Seidel swallowed, making an audible click in his throat. "What's this about?"

"I'm just here to talk about your tenant. The one in the place next door."

The tension drained out of Seidel's back and shoulders. He sighed and let his hands fall to his sides.

"Jesus H. Christ. You 'bout scared the piss out of me."

"What's the matter?" Loshak asked. "Don't like it when people let themselves into your place when you're not home?"

Finally, Seidel caught on. His brow wrinkled, and his mouth turned down in a scowl.

"Wait, FBI? I know who you are." He nodded his head as if he were acting in some low budget detective movie and just figured out the big twist. "You wanna talk about my renter. Or tenant or whatever you want to call it. You're the ex-husband, huh? That's what this is all about?"

Loshak nodded.

"Aw, hell," Seidel said, slumping. "Now I feel stupid. I got caught up in the, uh… you know, and, uh… Aw, shit. Fuck me. I apologize, man. Sincerely, I do. I never been a landlord before, but you should've heard some of the nightmare shit my mom had to put up with from her renters. It just felt like I was getting jerked around, you know? I wanted to stand up for myself, and I lost all perspective. Does that make sense?"

"We all make mistakes, Dan," Loshak said, showing the guy a cold, government smile. "It's not a problem. Not so long as it stops. Now. If there's any more trouble—"

"Oh, no way, there won't be," Seidel swore. "Believe me. I maybe ain't the brightest of bulbs, but I've never been one to make the same mistake twice."

CHAPTER 19

As he drove away, Loshak felt himself slump in the seat. He was exhausted. Going from reminiscing with Jan to thinking he was going to have to shoot that psycho landlord had really taken it out of him, not to mention the intense battle he'd done with the wooden planks of that damn deck.

It'd been worth it to see the guy almost pissing himself, though. He wished he could've recorded the whole thing for Jan. Give her back a little chuckle in return for all the peace of mind that asshole had taken away.

It was weird thinking he'd spent that whole time there in Jan's new house, in her new life. But nothing about his visit had felt weird at the time. The two of them had fallen right back into place, like neither of them had broken formation to begin with. It hadn't felt like everything was back to normal — nothing could ever go back to normal without Shelly; they were never going to stop missing her — but it also hadn't felt like everything was broken beyond repair anymore. Like…

Like what? Like he was going to get back together with Jan and ride off into the sunset?

Loshak snorted.

No, it was more like something inside him had loosened up, some muscle he hadn't realized he was tensing to the point that it quivered. It had relaxed the second Jan saw his face and smiled. She didn't hate him. It was strange, he thought, feeling incredible relief from a strain he didn't even know was there. Something life-affirming, something human and warm in the middle of an otherwise grisly trip to Florida.

Loshak checked his watch. He was supposed to ride along with the detectives following up on the bus station tipster — it seemed like a pretty solid lead — and they'd had to wait until after the kid got off basketball practice.

There was no way he'd make it back to the motel and then out to the Tamarac police station with enough time between for a nap, but he could stretch out in the TPD parking lot and grab some quick shuteye. He smiled at the thought, another pang of nostalgia firing in the emotional part of his brain — a nap in the car like back in his rookie days — but the smile was fleeting.

His mind circled quickly back to the facts of the case, his face going stern as his brain tried to work at that puzzle again, tried to understand the truth beyond those facts, like Spinks had talked about.

All the separate strands were still knotted up for now — tangled up in a mess that couldn't quite make sense — but the task force was poking at a lot of little snags now, a whole slew of little loops and angles to pick at. And surely one of them would pull loose and the whole thing would unravel in the killer's face. They were on his scent now. Closing in like a pack of coonhounds. Loshak could feel that. He thought maybe they all could. In so many ways, the case seemed about to break.

In addition to the bus station tip, there was the pawn shop angle, which was looking promising, too. If the guy was a serious junkie like he suspected, they might know something within the next day or so. Maybe even tonight.

As he wheeled into the parking lot of the Tamarac station, he caught a glimpse of himself in the rearview mirror. He was smiling.

Loshak realized that, for the first time in a long time, he was actually kind of excited to see how this all shook out. Not just dutiful. Not just doing his job to the best of his ability. Genuinely excited. Just like back in his rookie days.

CHAPTER 20

Evening was closing in on the man in black. He was still in the bar, the last holdover from the afternoon. Dmitri had long since disappeared, off to feed needles in some other dive for the night, and even the hangdog day bartender had changed shifts with a perky blonde in a pink tank top.

The barroom which had been nearly deserted earlier was bustling now with the after-work crowd, there to erase the spreadsheets and price checks and drain snakes from their minds with alcohol. Bodies in button-down shirts, flannel, scuffed and dirty work boots mixed and mingled with shiny high heels and dangly earrings, swarming over one another until they looked less like individuals and more like a single body with too many limbs, an endless human centipede, each face chomping up the shit the other faces spewed out.

Behold the lonely people. The vacant masses. They came out in droves to feel empty together. To try in vain to fill that void with any substance they happened upon. They all grinned like idiot apes, too. Probably to keep from crying.

The man in black watched them from his little table in the corner. Looking out at the crashing waves of humanity, but seeing the girl. That dramatic movie moment from the night before projected here in front of him. So real he felt like he could touch it.

The damsel in distress, thrashing in her bed.

Her pupils like black holes locking onto his face, staring into his eyes, looking right through him.

And then the headlights swinging over the walls of her room like searchlights. And the panic gripping him around the shoulders, grabbing him by the scruff of the neck.

The smash cut to him running like a pussy, like the little faggot his uncle always said he was. Not even man enough to finish off a little girl.

His bowels constricted at the memory, coiling into something tight and rigid.

The cocaine and the Budweiser dulled the self-loathing, but they weren't enough to kill it. It swirled in his gut, toxic and black, eating away at the pleasant bliss of the high until it was nothing, gone. Weak, helpless. It always came back to that, no matter what he did. He was helpless. Feeble. A limp dick of a human being.

"Waste," he mumbled to himself. A waste of space, waste of breath, waste of life. "Fuck!" He slammed his open palm on the tabletop, the sound lost in the pounding surf of humanity screaming all around him.

How many of those blabbering shitfaces had any inkling of what real power was? They slept and worked and watched TV. Served some master, some society their whole lives long. Domesticated animals, all of them. And for what? A house in the suburbs? A slot in some corporation? Dreams of walk-in closets and stainless steel appliances?

Meanwhile, across the room from this mindless herd, sat one who held the power over life and death in his hands. He was the Other, the demon child with the sacrificial knife, the last face you saw in the night, the reaper no walls could protect you from.

He was their worst fucking nightmare.

And none of them felt his presence. None of them realized they were standing within arm's reach of Death.

They chewed their cud, drank their swill, slow blinking and docile as ever. Cattle just waiting to be steered down the kill chute.

His beer was empty again, but the coke was keeping him high enough that he found himself at the bar without any transition shots. He told the perky blonde in the pink tank top he wanted another Budweiser.

While she turned around to get it, he imagined jumping over the bar, slipping up behind her and wrapping that lamp cord around her throat. This time he wouldn't pussy out. Not a chance. He would strangle her with everyone here watching, witnesses to an animal who couldn't be tamed, to his supreme power over life and death.

"Here you go," the blonde said cheerfully, sliding the bottle across the sticky wood.

The man in black picked it up and turned, expecting the jump cut back to his table. Instead, his elbow and hand were smacked off course halfway by a massive arm. The bottle tumbled from his fingers, crashing to the floor. Brown glass shattered. White suds poured out the jagged remainder of the neck.

"Oh shit." The arm was talking to him. It was attached to this enormous pro-wrestler-looking fuck with a sunburn and bleached blond hair spiked straight up.

The pro-wrestler grinned as he sized up the man in black, then the broken bottle at their feet. The pro-wrestler's teeth were huge and unnaturally white, like squares of that blister pack gum jammed into his face.

"Nice hands, Feet." The pro-wrestler grabbed the man in black's shoulder with one warm, damp paw. "Maybe watch where you're going next time and shit."

The man in black flinched under the contact, his skin crawling, his brain sending out frantic signals to run, escape, flee, get the fuck away.

The pro-wrestler saw it, narrowed his eyes a little at that moment of panic flashing over the man in black's face. He started to laugh.

"Don't shit yourself, little guy. I'm not gonna hurt you! Not unless you fuck with me." He squeezed the man in black's shoulder until it hurt, shaking him around a little just to show everyone that he could. To prove that the man in black was the weakling, the lesser being. Laughing the whole time. Grinning with those blister pack gum teeth out in everybody's face. "And you're not gonna fuck with me, are you? Are you?"

Blood pounded in the man in black's temples. He couldn't get loose. He jerked at his whole body, trying to pull free, but he couldn't. This asshole was crushing his shoulder, trapping him, hurting him, and he couldn't do a fucking thing about it.

"Nah, you're not gonna fuck with anybody." The pro-wrestler gave the man in black a shove, pushing down as he let go and dragging his fat, wet fingers over the man in black's shirt. "Get outta here."

The man in black stumbled a few steps before he could stand up straight. His face had been numb most of the night, but now he could feel it burning, hot circles like brands high on his cheeks. He spun around, backing up out of reach of the pro-wrestler's wet sausage fingers.

But the asshole was already going the other way, slanting his wide shoulders through the sea of humanity like an overhead view of a sinking ocean liner headed straight to the bottom. A second later, the waves swallowed him up.

CHAPTER 21

Loshak sat in the kitchen of a modern ranch-style house with the mousy Detective Renaud, across the table from the young bus station tipster. Not directly across, though. Loshak had been careful to take the seat to the left of that one when they sat down, not wanting to start off the interview in a position most young males instinctively read as aggressive or antagonistic.

Andrew Jackson — who they'd already established preferred to be called Drew, for obvious reasons — was fifteen, on the short side, probably a guard or an undersized small forward on the junior varsity basketball team, and he needed a shower. He was still in his gym clothes, and he smelled like the inside of a locker room, even across the table. A pungent, almost swampy odor, Loshak thought. Apparently when Renaud had said they were setting up this interview after basketball practice, he'd meant immediately after.

Drew's mother, a Mrs. Kathy Jackson, hovered by the huge stainless-steel fridge, arms crossed over her chest, clenched tightly to her body in a defensive posture as if she were afraid they planned to beat the details out of her son.

"So, Drew," Loshak said, leaning an elbow on the table. "We understand you overheard someone – a man – make a claim that might be related to the case we're working. Can you kind of start at the beginning and run us through exactly what happened?"

Drew shrugged. "Yeah. Me and my friend were passing by the bus station the other day when—"

"I told you I didn't want you hanging around that place," Mrs. Jackson said, plucking at the sleeve of her fuzzy white sweater. "It's nothing but a bunch of bums and lowlifes down there."

"I wasn't hanging around!" Drew sighed. "We just stopped to grab some McMuffins on the way to school, and it's like one big parking lot between McDonald's and the bus station. What do you want me to do? Walk all the way around town?"

"Are you serious right now? McDonald's? You know I don't give you lunch money just so you can go buy that garbage—"

"Ma'am," Loshak said before the argument could escalate any further. "I know you're only trying to be a good mom, but we really need to get Drew's story with as little interruption as possible."

Mrs. Jackson raised her hands. "I'm sorry. It's just that... McDonald's? That's all corn syrup and saturated fat. I guess you can see whether diabetes or heart disease hits first. Drew, we've talked about this a thousand times."

"More like you yelled about it," Drew mumbled, scraping dirt from under his thumbnail.

"Obviously not loud enough."

"If you wouldn't mind, ma'am," Loshak said.

"Right, of course." Mrs. Jackson went around behind the granite-topped island and sat on one of the stools. She gestured for them to continue.

Detective Renaud cleared his throat. "You said you and a friend were passing the station... What's your friend's name?"

"Kenny," Drew said. Then after a second, he must've realized they weren't on intimate terms with all of the Kennys in the Miami area because he added, "Kenny Lopez. He's in my class."

Behind the island, Mrs. Jackson's eyes narrowed, mouth screwed up in a sour frown. Not a big Kenny fan, apparently. Before she could get started again, Loshak shot her a warning look.

She stood up, raising her hands as if he were pointing a gun at her, and stepped through the doorway into the dining room.

"Did Kenny overhear this guy talking as well?" Loshak asked.

Drew nodded. "I wanted to tell someone right away. Like, call the police — you guys — right then. But Kenny said we didn't want people thinking we were snitches."

Mrs. Jackson's scoff was audible even from a room away. Loshak stifled the urge to roll his eyes.

"Plus, this guy we heard, he's not really a scary guy," Drew went on, his voice gaining conviction, as if he were trying to prove his mom was overreacting. "Like, he doesn't seem like the kind of guy who'd actually kill somebody. He's too nice, you know. Smiling and stuff. Like a what do you call it? A people person."

"So you know this guy?" Renaud asked. "The man you overheard claiming responsibility for the killings?"

"Uh…" Drew glanced at the doorway. "No. I don't know him."

Renaud glanced at Loshak. Loshak stood up and stretched as if his back was getting stiff. He didn't have to pretend too hard; after that nap in the car and sitting for so long, his back actually was getting sore. Instead of going back to his seat, however, Loshak leaned against the doorjamb, blocking the kid's view of his mom.

"Are you sure you've never seen this guy before?" Detective Renaud asked. "A minute ago, it sounded like he was kind of familiar to you. At least a little."

Drew's eyes flicked to the doorway again. Loshak gave him a friendly smile. The kid looked back at Renaud.

"I might've seen him around once or twice," he said.

"Hanging around the depot?" Renaud leaned forward in his seat. "Or do you know him from somewhere else?"

"The depot mostly."

"Know his name?"

Drew licked his lips.

"I don't really remember." He glanced down at the table. "Maybe… Larry?"

A wall of fuzzy white shoved past Loshak, knocking him out of the way.

"Larry the wino?!" Mrs. Jackson snapped, hands on her hips.

Loshak had to move to the side to see around the angry mom. Drew was refusing to look up from the table.

"Larry who?" Renaud asked, looking from mother to son.

"Look at me, Drew. That's who you're talking about, isn't it?" Mrs. Jackson demanded.

The kid barely met her eyes. He nodded.

"You and that Kenny were skipping school again, weren't you? You told me that call I got from the school was a mistake — that you were late and Mr. Greenwell forgot to mark you off the absentee form. But you were skipping school down at the depot, trying to get one of those bums to buy booze for you, weren't you?"

"No!"

"I can't believe this!" Mrs. Jackson was shaking her head. "Well, you can just forget about Friday, mister."

"What?! That's bullcrap!"

"And if you think for one second I won't take away your permit—"

A vein stood out in Drew's neck. "I wasn't trying to get anybody to buy—"

"Excuse me," Loshak said, stepping between them and raising his voice to be heard over their shouting. "Hey, FBI guy here. Working a murder case."

The Jacksons fell silent, looking at him.

"We need to know this guy's name. You said it was Larry something?"

Mother and son stared each other down for a tense moment before the mom broke the silence.

"Larry the Wino," Mrs. Jackson said, plucking at her fuzzy white sleeves. "He hangs around the depot. Been there for as long as I can remember. He's a drunk and a loser, and I've told my son to *stay away from him.*"

Drew opened his mouth, but Loshak cut him off.

"Do you know his last name?" Loshak doubted she did given the circumstances, but he wanted to head the two of them off before they got going again.

"No," Mrs. Jackson snapped.

Detective Renaud turned to Drew. "Can you tell me what Larry the Wino said about the murders?"

Drew shrugged, picking at his thumbnail again. "He

had this knife on him. One of those folding ones. He pulled it out and said that was what he used to cut their throats."

CHAPTER 22

The man in black waited outside the bar, tucked in the shadows like the predator he was, his back to the painted brick. Waiting. Hunting. His teeth gritted so hard his jaw ached. His breath hissed in and out, each exhale extra-long, almost a growl. Hatred and humiliation thudded inside his skull, bright red and pulsating in time with his thundering heart.

The asphalt was all wet out here in the parking lot, slick and black in a way that reminded him of playing in the rain when he was a kid, reminded him of gutters and sewers and potholes full of muddy water. But he smelled none of these things. Not rain or sewage or that dry-spit smell the air got when the mugginess hit its peak level of misery.

No. He smelled blood.

He always smelled blood when he was angry. A metallic stench, almost like rust, he thought, but not quite. Wetter than that. And bodily. The odor existed only in his head, of course. Not really there. Just another figment banging around up there in the ol' brain pan with all the other fucked up movies of things he'd seen and done.

And he imagined that pro-wrestler-looking asshat coming outside, strutting toward the parking lot, his giant block-shaped head still full of what a big shit he was because he could shove people around.

And the man in black would slide up behind him, on Death's silent feet, and shove his knife through the knot of muscle and tissue at the back of that ropy neck, into the spinal column, slitting straight up into the brainstem, or giving it a good fucking try, at least. And he'd watch the muscle-bound oaf drop to the ground, eyes going wide, face turning redder and redder as he realized his lungs didn't work anymore. Face going purple. Then going gray. Little choked gasps pouring out of his lips.

But no, the fucker would just say it'd been a sneak attack, that his foe didn't have the balls to take him on face-to-face.

No, what the man in black would do was go right up to him, give his shoulders a little feint to get the guy thinking he was going for a headshot, and then he'd jam his blade deep into the abdominal cavity — the wide open body shot that was typically there in a street fight when everyone was thinking about Hollywood haymakers. Giving the knife a good, hard rip to the side would spill all the gut works right out like wet noodles dumped into a colander. And while he was grabbing at his insides, trying to hold his life in with nothing but his fat sausage fingers, the man in black would stab him in the balls. Pop both of his grapes and pin his sack to his taint. Then who wouldn't have the balls, huh?

He waited, hand on the knife in his pocket. The handle was warm to the touch. Ready to penetrate. Ready to carve. Ready to plant in that fucker's asshole, slice him open all the way around like an orange peel – up the back, over the head, down the face, through the chest and stomach and groin – and kick the halves apart so all the slices fell in a heap on the dirty pavement. Ready to peel all of his skin off, to get a look at the red stringy bits all close up, to see the way they looked like all the rest.

It was true what they said, he thought. We're all the same on the inside. Red and wet. Meat.

The man in black licked his lips as he watched the splatterpunk scenes play out in his imagination. The beer and coke were still sizzling their electricity around inside his head, keeping him sharp. Ready for the kill.

The door to the bar swung open, letting a driving guitar riff and the sounds of drinking and shouting and some woman's high-pitched giggle out into the night.

Enormous shoulders filled the door frame. Fat head. Spiked hair. The pro-wrestler stepped out into the night.

CHAPTER 23

"Are they going to send someone to canvass the bus station?" Spinks asked, pointing his key fob over his shoulder and locking his car.

"Well, yeah." Loshak glanced up and down the street to make sure they could cross over to the pawn shop safely.

It was deep evening, and there were headlights in both directions, but far enough away that they could make it. He started walking, then pushed it into a half-jog.

"They're sending a sketch artist to work with the kid and his friend, so the uniforms'll have something to show around in case the name doesn't ring any bells."

"Damn." The reporter snapped his fingers. "Too bad we don't already have that sketch."

Loshak stepped up onto the sidewalk, the blinking neon sign overhead bathing him in pale green. Spinks' loafers hit the cement half a beat after his. The pawn shop angle had turned up this potential hit — South McPike's Pawn — a little over fifteen minutes from the Iverson crime scene. Nobody had been to canvass it yet, but the Pinecrest PD had gotten an emergency call that morning while the task force was meeting regarding a fight between the owner and a strange, nervous guy trying to sell stuff. Uniforms had shown up, but by then the guy was gone.

Since Spinks hadn't been able to ride along to the interview with the bus station kid, Loshak gave him a call afterward to see if he wanted to follow up on the pawn shop angle.

"Maybe not," Loshak said. "If this guy turns out to be legit, if he actually interacted with our killer and it wasn't just some random colorful character, then we can have him sit down with a sketch artist, too—"

"And see if their pictures line up," Spinks finished for him, nodding excitedly. "All right, yeah. Let's do this."

He opened the pawn shop's door, eliciting a robotic chime from overhead, and gestured for Loshak to go ahead.

The inside of the pawn shop was lit with bright fluorescents, rendering every inch of the glass countertops, hanging guitars, and weird pieces of pop art in harsh white light. A young, heavy-set woman behind the counter was arranging an assortment of swords in a tabletop display, but otherwise, the shop was deserted.

"Excuse me, miss," Loshak said to her, digging his badge out of his jacket. "Agent Loshak, FBI. I'm here to speak with Jason McPike."

"Yeah, just a sec." She set the last sword in the brackets, then lowered a hinged metal arm over the top and locked them in place with a key from the ring hanging around her neck. "I'll get him."

She disappeared around a corner, the keys patting against her chest as she went.

"Weird," Spinks said.

Loshak looked at him. "Her?"

"No, that." Spinks pointed at the display. "They've got katanas and US Cavalry swords and a rapier, and I'm pretty sure that one's a falchion. That's like a seven-century spread. Weird that they'd put them all in one rack."

"Sword enthusiast?" Loshak asked, a hint of a smile

pulling at his lips.

Spinks chuckled. "Like you've never watched *Pawn Stars*."

A big guy, broad as a truck, came around the corner from the back. He was the kind of obese that looked awkward, as if the fat was holding his shoulders and arms at a weird, boxy angle. Loshak couldn't tell whether the guy was already on the defensive or if that was just the way he was built.

"Mr. McPike?"

"You guys the feds?" he asked, a hint of Midwestern accent.

"I am. He's consulting." Loshak nodded at Spinks. "Are you the owner here?"

"Yeah." Defensive, definitely.

Spinks leaned his elbows on the counter. "We're not here to bust you for anything — except maybe filing your swords weirdly." He waved a hand at the rack. "Seriously, this anachronism doesn't bother anybody but me?"

McPike snorted, and his big shoulders dropped an inch. "Look, I get it. You've seen *Pawn Stars*. Now, would it be rude to ask what you all are here about?"

"Did one of your customers call the cops the other day because an altercation broke out in your store?" Loshak said.

McPike's round head fell into a nod as he began to speak.

"Yeah, some chick got scared when this little crackhead started throwing a fit in here," McPike said, looking down his nose at Loshak. "He was pissed that I wouldn't buy any of his crap, but it was just cheap trash. I told him how it was. He got agitated, started yelling about how valuable his little junk heap was, having a little conniption fit or whatever the hell. I told him to git. He wouldn't. I threw him out. End of story."

Loshak slipped a piece of paper out of his jacket and handed it to McPike. "Do you remember if this guy was trying to sell anything on this list?"

For a few seconds, McPike scanned in silence. Then he took a big breath and nodded and set the sheet on the counter.

"Spoons," he said, tapping the page. "That little weirdo was trying to sell me a fistful of cheap costume jewelry and a bunch of spoons. Getting all hot and bothered about it, too, like I said."

Loshak's brow furrowed. "What kind of spoons?"

McPike just looked at him for a second.

"The kind you eat with."

Spinks laughed. "Not the kind you rednecks like to play music with?"

This wrung another snort out of the big guy.

"I mean they were spoons," he said, turning his hands over to show his wide, pink palms. "Just soups spoons and teaspoons and whatever."

"Were they ornamental?" Loshak asked. "Real silver?"

"No, just regular stainless steel. They weren't even a set. And they were all dinged up and scratched. Looked like junk someone purchased at Kmart circa 1987."

Loshak looked at Spinks. The reporter twitched his eyebrows upward, then turned back to the pawn shop owner.

"You wouldn't happen to have the tapes from those

security cameras, would you?"

CHAPTER 24

By the time they left the pawn shop, it was late. Dark. Loshak was more than ready to call it a night, crawl into his undersized motel bed, wrap himself in a makeshift cocoon of scratchy blankets and hibernate for a good long while. He leaned back in the passenger seat of Spinks' car and let the headrest cradle his skull.

"We were close. Can't believe the cameras were down," Spinks said.

Loshak shrugged.

"At a lot of these places, the cameras are for show," the agent said. "Of course, I find the pawn shop owners to be on the paranoid side in general. A lot of 'em wear a gun on their hip as they work. You'd think of all people, they'd be the most vigilant about the security."

"Down for maintenance, the dude said. You think that was for real?"

"Who knows? Guess it doesn't matter much."

"Yeah," Spinks agreed with a sigh. "Guess not."

Neon lights and palm trees embellished the landscape outside. The city teemed with life, ready to bustle deep into the night. It must be a weekend, Loshak realized. He thought about it. Yeah, it was Friday.

"So no big plans tonight?" he said. "Every reporter I've ever known spent his Friday nights holed up in a bar somewhere."

Spinks smirked.

"Nah. I mean, I used to go out, but... I kind of changed my habits after, you know, Davin."

Shit. Loshak had stepped into it again. He couldn't help but feel that he should be more careful in what he said to Spinks.

"Yeah, that has a way of changing things," the agent said, trying to keep his tone light.

"Drinking, socializing, those things have their place in life, but they're a way to relax, you know?" Spinks said. "A way to find a little relief. And me? I always feel pressed for time. I guess I'd rather work, exert myself, accomplish something. Relaxing just doesn't fill my tank up. Doesn't make me feel any better. I'd rather seek satisfaction."

"Well, I know how that is, believe me," Loshak said. "Might know it a little too well, to be honest with you. My ex-wife would tell you the same."

They pulled to a stop at a red light, all the downtown activity swirling around the car.

"I had to be the strong one after Davin died, and that was fine. Someone had to hold things together. Might as well be me."

Spinks propped an elbow on the armrest while they waited for the light to turn.

"But about six or eight months later, I started falling off. Descending. That's how depression feels to me. You're slowly sinking into this quiet place, this numbed out nothing place. Into this rut that has some kind of suction power to hold you down there."

Loshak nodded. He'd never fallen all the way in, but he'd gotten a glimpse here and there when Shelly was sick and in the months after she died.

"You're in pain there, but I think more than that, you're distant from everything outside yourself. You disappear within the walls of your skull, somehow pulled deeper in like a turtle retracting into its shell."

The light turned green, and the car lurched into motion again.

"Shit snuck up on me, too. Sucker punched me in the gut a few times before I ever realized it was there. Next thing I knew, I'd been down in this hole for weeks, maybe for months. And I mean all the way down. Touching bottom. Hurting all the time. Daydreaming about offing myself. Shit like that."

Spinks went quiet for a minute, rubbing his forehead, perhaps reliving those dark thoughts for a moment.

"So I said to myself, 'Shit, I gotta do something about this.' Started trying everything I could think of. Energy therapy lamps, where you sit in bright light for 15 or 20 minutes first thing in the morning. I got myself a gravity blanket. You heard of them?"

Loshak's brow furrowed. It sounded like something an astronaut might use.

"Can't say that I have."

"It's this weighted blanket. Sort of hugs you at night more or less. Supposed to help with anxiety and the like."

"Did it work?" Loshak asked.

Spinks' head bobbled from side to side.

"Yeah, I mean… they both helped. The light, the blanket. So I finally talked to a doctor. Tried out some different medications. Found something that worked there, too. But I think above all, I figured out that I'm a guy who wants to go hard while I'm still here. I wanted to live, to really live, so I had to fight the depression off, and I had to get back to attacking life, you know? I have to get hands-on, get assertive, maybe sometimes aggressive," he said, squeezing his fingers into a fist and shaking it in the air. "That's my nature. I'm hard-wired that way."

Spinks relaxed his hand, let it fall into his lap, and lifted his chin.

"I think you have to live in today. Have to embrace it. Have to do something with it. Because one of these Todays will be the last one. No tomorrow. That's about the only certainty there is in life."

He turned his gaze on Loshak.

"You and I know that better than most anyone, right? And not only because of Davin and Shelly. Our jobs put us face to face with murders and sudden deaths. So many abrupt endings, brutal endings. Just look at these people in the case we're working now. They head to bed one night, and that's the end of their story. No more. One way or another, it'll happen that way for you, happen that way for me."

Eyes swiveling back to the windshield, Spinks stared out into the darkness of the night and shook his head.

"No matter who you are, there's a final day, and then your life shears off into nothing. I just want to really live right up to the end, you know?"

CHAPTER 25

Loshak kicked off his shoes and sank onto the motel bed with a sigh of relief. It'd been a long one, but productive. Probably all the more exhausting thanks to the muggy Florida air that pressed the heat under his clothes, smeared it directly on his skin with its moist touch, enveloped him everywhere he went.

The window unit AC worked against the humidity now. Beat it back little by little. The thing churned out an awful noise like a growling jet engine and rattled against its frame with little snaps and cracks, but it kicked out an impressive gust of cool dry air that Loshak had angled via the slatted vent to blow right at him.

He closed his eyes, felt the cool wind seep into his skin, and thought back over the new information.

Even with all their bickering, the bus station kid and his mom were going to be a huge help, one way or the other. It almost seemed too good to be true. The guy had even shown them the possible murder weapon, for Christ's sake. The pawn shop guy had given them great intel, too, of course. That lead had soured a little there at the end when they found out the shop's camera system had been down for an update that morning, but the owner had agreed to talk to a sketch artist and give her what he remembered about the spoon guy. Between both descriptions, they would come up with something usable that they could get to the news outlets around Miami.

And then there was the bludgeoned girl, Mary Iverson, still recovering in the hospital. With any luck, she could provide them with yet another description. An up close and personal one, at that.

Loshak felt some of the muscles in his back slowly release, the tension of the daily grind finally relenting. And the sweat that had sogged his crevices and temples for most of the day seemed to have dried as well. These feelings came with a strange euphoria. It felt incredible to simply be dry and cool for a little bit.

He longed for sleep, for the deepest levels of unconsciousness, and he knew it would come to him soon. Quickly, he thought. All at once.

Even while he was grabbing some shut-eye tonight, work on the case would continue. At this very moment, uniforms were staking out the bus station and pawn shops near South McPike's that their killer was likely to try. They'd be at it around the clock.

Loshak rolled onto his side, letting the AC blow on his shoulder blades some, feeling another wave of that bliss wash over him.

He was glad he'd decided to stick around and see this through. He felt like they were getting somewhere. And Jan. He'd been able to do something useful, had helped her out in her new life. It felt good.

He settled back onto the pillows and stretched out, letting his mind wander. He and Spinks made a good team. The reporter had a natural talent for engaging people, getting them to open up. Loshak could understand them, see what their motivations were in any situation given enough time, but he couldn't always connect with them or

145

persuade them the way Spinks seemed to be able to. Maybe there was something there that he could learn, some skill or trick or approach to glean in the way the reporter handled himself.

On the way back from the pawn shop, Spinks had gotten Loshak to open up about Jan and the situation with her landlord. The reporter said he had a friend down at the county clerk's office, offered to have them poke around and see if the rat-killing landlord, Seidel, had any other properties. If he did, he might have other tenants, maybe even a history of complaints. Enough digging could turn up something they could charge this guy with. More leverage to use against him.

Loshak felt himself drifting off. The motel might be cheap, but the bed beat the hell out of kicking back the seat in a rental car. The light on the nightstand was still on, and he was fully dressed and lying on top of the blankets, but his brain had decided it was time to shut down. He didn't fight it.

There was a dream then, images and words that slipped away from him, leaving behind this dull ache in his chest. Not quite sadness, he thought. More like nostalgia. A longing for something that he couldn't remember, for something he couldn't have, Not anymore. Not ever again.

Then there was a sound. Shrill. Almost a scream.

His phone.

Loshak rolled up onto his elbow and grabbed his phone off the nightstand with hands that felt like they were made of wood. He stared at the thing. Had to blink a few times before his eyes would focus on the screen, process what he saw there. He didn't recognize the number, but the area code was local to Miami.

He thumbed the answer icon. "Agent Loshak."

"We got him."

It took a second for Loshak to place the voice. At first, all he could think was what he'd first heard it say: *Hey-hey, somebody had a good idea.* The image of a badge followed, hanging from a mousy guy's neck and stamped with the name Detective Lynn Renaud.

Loshak rubbed at his eyes with his free hand. "Got who?"

"The creep from the bus station," Renaud said. "We got him."

CHAPTER 26

An hour later, Loshak and Spinks were sitting in the Tamarac PD's observation room, watching the interrogation room on a tv monitor. Detective Hwang, a chunky woman on the uphill side of middle age, was questioning their bus station guy, Larry the Wino.

"All right, to start off with, can you give me your name, age, and address?" Hwang asked, her tone friendly. It was a standard opener, the sort of stuff he wouldn't have any reason to lie about.

"Sure, yeah." He rocked in his seat, like a full-body nod, then scrubbed his hands together like an overgrown rodent. "Lawrence Bevacqua — Larry, for short. Forty-nine years young."

He grinned at his joke, showing the detective a mouthful of booze- and nicotine-stained teeth.

"I'm not really at a mailing address right now. Between homes, you could say. My bud, Dennis, lets me stay on the couch on his porch, but it's not, like, a permanent thing."

"Oh yeah?" Hwang said, politely interested. "Where's that at?"

"Over on Cranberry Street. 4971."

"Oh, okay," the detective said as if she knew the house. Then she looked up from her notes. "Are you hungry, Larry? Or maybe thirsty? I know it's late, but there's a vending machine down the hall. I could grab you a snack."

"Well, yeah, I could eat."

"It's mostly Mars Bars and Snickers, but there's a packet of Cheez-Its in there, too. Got a preference?"

"I like the Snickers when I can get 'em," Bevacqua said.

Hwang smiled at him. "Back in a sec."

While the detective stepped out, Loshak watched Bevacqua. Open body language. No crossed arms or nervous leg-shaking. He just sat there, looking around the interrogation room, mildly interested, the tiniest smile curling the corners of his lips. All fun and games for this one, Loshak thought. So far, at least.

The door of the observation room opened, and Hwang leaned in, grabbing the Snickers off the table. The Cheez-Its and Mars Bar she left behind. She gave Loshak and Spinks a little salute with the bar, then left.

A few seconds later, she reappeared on the screen, shutting the interrogation room door behind her.

"Here you go." She handed the candy bar to Bevacqua before sitting back down in her chair. "Honestly, I never really saw the appeal of Snickers. I like a soft candy bar, like Three Musketeers."

"See? I didn't take you for the whipped nougat type. Not at all. But I'm gonna tell you flat out right here and now, you got it all wrong." Bevacqua peeled open the Snickers and took a bite, talking between chews. "You get more full when you've got something to really chew on. You crunch on those peanuts and your mouth thinks, 'I must be getting a lot of food if I'm having to work so hard.' Then your gut gets the message and thinks it's had a full meal. We're hardwired for that crunchy texture, you know? The mouth craves it."

Hwang shook her head in good-natured disagreement.

"If I want crunchy, I'm going for something salty, you know? Pretzels, that kind of thing."

"No way." Bevacqua waved a dismissive hand at her. "Pretzels can go to hell. Directly to hell. Do not pass go. For salty, you want corn chips."

Hwang laughed. "Not me!"

While they chatted, Loshak admired the detective's easy friendliness. Like the offered snack, the whole conversation was one big maneuver designed to put Bevacqua at ease. Make him feel like this was just friendly small talk. They both liked snack foods, they must both be on the same side, even if they couldn't agree on which ones were the best.

They settled back down, but Hwang retained the friendly tone.

"So, Larry, can you tell me where you were last night?"

"I was at the bar over on Cranberry, having a drink," he said.

"With a friend? Dennis, maybe?"

"No, not last night. I was by myself."

"Did you talk to anyone who might remember you there?"

Bevacqua's smile slipped as he started to realize this wasn't just a friendly chat about candy bars.

"I don't remember talking to anybody," he said. "But the bartender and me go way back. He can probably vouch. Horatio's his name. Good guy. Stand-up guy."

"What time did you leave?" Hwang asked, still nothing confrontational in her voice.

"Last call, when they kick everybody out." Bevacqua hooked a thumb over his shoulder. "I hit the road, Jack. Headed to my home-sweet-couch to sleep it off."

The detective jotted this down, then crossed her legs and leaned forward.

"I'm sure you've seen the stuff about the killings in the news?" She phrased it like a question.

"Of course, yeah." Still lots of open body language, Loshak noted, and he wasn't avoiding eye contact. "I mean, who hasn't? It's all over the place."

"What d'you think motivates somebody to do something like that? Kill innocent people in their homes?"

Bevacqua hesitated. "I don't… I honestly don't know."

Beside Loshak, Spinks snorted.

"Oh, I think you do, you creepy son of a bitch."

Loshak turned his attention back to the screen, frowning.

"No idea?" Detective Hwang was asking. "I thought maybe you'd have some insight. You seem like you know a thing or two about the world."

"I guess he must be pretty sick." Bevacqua shrugged. "You'd have to be to murder a whole family, right? With kids, too? And raping an old lady? That's not… that's not normal."

He shook his head, frowning as he spoke. "I tell ya, there's been a few nights, sleeping out on that porch, with just a thin layer of window screens between me and the rest of the world…" He paused, then gave a nervous laugh. "It's a little scary to think about."

Detective Hwang nodded, smiling. "I can imagine."

On the screen, the door to the interrogation room opened again, drawing both Bevacqua's and Hwang's attention.

Detective Renaud leaned in. "Hey, sorry to interrupt,

but you got a phone call. Can't wait."

Hwang stood up.

"Excuse me, Larry, I'll be right back." She followed Renaud off the screen, pulling the door shut on her way out.

A few seconds later, she rejoined Loshak and Spinks in the observation room. The three of them watched the small, homeless guy chewing over his Snickers bar.

"What do you think?" Hwang asked.

"His hand's shaking," Spinks said, pointing. Onscreen, Bevacqua was raising a Styrofoam cup of water to his lips. "He's scared."

Loshak shook his head. "Not with the way he's leaning back in his seat relaxing. Probably tremors."

"He does smell like the dumpster behind a liquor store," Hwang said.

They watched him lick a ribbon of caramel off his thumb.

"I don't like it," Loshak said. "He's too relaxed."

Hwang went back into the interrogation room and sat down across from their suspect.

"Sorry about that," she said, shuffling her papers. "So, do you ever go over to the bus station, Larry?"

"Oh yeah, I go down there and hang out. Shoot the shit. There's always something happening at the bus station."

"What kind of shit?" the detective asked.

"Pardon?"

"You said you go down there to shoot the shit. What kind of things do you talk about?

"Well, this and that," Bevacqua said, shrugging one shoulder. "You know. Whatever's rolling through my skull kind of spills right out when I open my mouth, but…. Kinda hard to think of specifics off the top of my head."

"Have the murders ever come up as a topic of discussion?"

Bevacqua licked his lips. Loshak zeroed in on the motion, leaning closer to the monitor almost unconsciously. Their suspect was making a show of really thinking on Hwang's question. Frowning, bobbing his head from side to side as if this were a real puzzler.

"Yeah, it might've come up," he finally said.

"But you can't think of any specifics?" Hwang asked, her tone doubtful. A little patronizing.

Bevacqua folded his arms. "Not really."

"Because we have a witness from the bus station who says you were bragging about the killings."

Bevacqua shook his head.

"No?" Hwang asked, raising an eyebrow. Her eyes darted down at her notepad. "You didn't say, quote, 'I slit the one lady's throat and the blood, man, it gushed out like cherry Kool-Aid?'"

"I don't…" He trailed off. "I can't really say."

"You can't say?" All the friendliness was gone. Loshak could almost feel the chill rolling off Hwang. "Or you don't want to say because you know if you confess you're headed straight to Bradford County?"

"I didn't—"

"Because you'll get the death penalty for sure, Larry. No doubt in my mind. Unless you tell me what happened. A full confession can go a long way," Hwang said. "Give me a full confession right here, right now, and the prosecutor could probably be convinced to take death off the table.

Compliance would be met with mercy, but only if you're straight with us from the start. It's up to you."

Bevacqua shifted in his seat, one leg jiggling under the table. He wiped his hands down his stubbly face.

Hwang leaned in closer. "You know the lethal injection is standard at this point, but you can still go to the chair by request. Did you know that?"

Bevacqua wasn't making eye contact anymore, but the detective kept working this angle.

"I gotta say, the chair would be kinda tempting," she said. "It's more iconic. Dramatic. It'll make sure you go out with a bang. Or should I say a jolt?" She tutted her tongue once and shook her head. "The needle is the pussy way out, if you ask me. Which one are you gonna pick, Larry? Needle or chair? Which way do you want to go?"

"Okay, look!" Bevacqua's voice cracked. "I was just…"

His shoulders sagged, and he deflated. It made him look seventy instead of forty-nine.

"I was just talkin' shit. I do that sometimes, run my mouth, but I never killed nobody."

There was a loud, wet snork from the interrogation room, and Loshak realized Bevacqua had started to cry.

"I'm sorry." He scrubbed his filthy sleeve across his nose. "I was just messing, you know. Messing around. I didn't think anyone would take me seriously."

CHAPTER 27

The big, pro-wrestler-looking fuck weaved across the wet, black asphalt of the parking lot, fumbling with his key ring. He half-hummed, half-sang under his breath as he went, oblivious to the shadow creeping along behind him.

Two rows back from the bar, a silver crossover blipped, and its headlights flickered. The guy corrected course toward it.

His shadow, the man in black, followed, his shoulders a little hunched, arms splayed at his sides.

He moved without sound. Light on his feet. Darting little steps that closed the gap between the two figures quickly.

Electricity thrummed in his chest, in his head. Little arcs of it shooting all through him. Lighting him up inside.

And he sucked in a silent breath as he moved to within an arm's length of the big motherfucker. Mouth wet. Teeth bared. Lungs greedy for oxygen with which to propel him through this next part.

He did not think now. He no longer needed to. He acted on instinct, on autopilot.

Dark impulses moved him along. Shadows in his head that whispered without words, that pushed him on to the next thing. They told him everything he needed to know.

They told him how to move, how to breathe, where to step, when to raise the blade, how to angle his body as though these instructions for murder were a radio wave beamed into his skull, a station broadcasting live, straight out of hell. Playing all the hits.

And now he was there.

Close enough to touch him.

Body coiled.

Ready to strike.

Ready to kill.

I am destruction.

The pro-wrestler snorted at something as he opened his door, shaking his head, and then he plopped himself into the driver's seat, bouncing once before he settled in for good.

He looked funny sitting down, the incongruence of his physique coming clear. The bulk of the upper body revealed itself to be in sharp contrast to the little stick legs, the bony knees straining at the fabric of his pants. Someone had been skipping leg day altogether from the looks of it.

Absurd.

Cartoonish.

It almost made the man in black laugh, almost broke the tension, almost snapped him out of the psychotic trance he had fallen into.

Almost.

The big oaf was reaching for the door when he saw the man in black. And his knife.

The wrestler did a double take, eyes locking on the blade. Stretching wider. Mouth falling open to match.

His eyebrows jumped up his forehead. Two frightened brown caterpillars leaping for the bleached blonde spikes above.

And the man in black lashed out, a powerful forward

thrust that planted the blade in the pro-wrestler's throat, then he ripped it to the side, opening a gaping hole in his neck.

The pro-wrestler blinked. Gagged. Eyes and mouth now opened about as wide as they could go. Yawning like the wound where his neck used to be.

Wet, slurping sounds came out of the broken hole in the throat, sounds that made the man in black think of sucking the last inch of frozen sugar out of an Icee.

Blood sprayed out in a strange spiral like a broken jet in a jacuzzi, drizzling down the steering wheel, sluicing all over the dash. And little coils of steam twirled away from the dark liquid. It almost looked like fresh-brewed coffee in the half-light. Hot and ready.

The pro-wrestler's hands patted at the wound, dumb and helpless, his fat sausage fingers dripping red, redirecting the spray.

His eyes were wide like a scared child's. Blinking. Staring out at nothing. Defeated. The light already draining from them.

The man in black grinned. Wasn't so tough now, was he?

CHAPTER 28

Detective Hwang returned to the observation room with Detective Renaud tagging along. Loshak scooted his chair back and rested his ankle on his knee. Spinks perched on the corner of the table, arms crossed.

"Well?" Renaud asked, looking from his partner to Loshak and Spinks.

"I don't think Bevacqua's our guy," Hwang said.

Loshak shook his head. "I don't think so, either."

"What are you guys talking about?" Spinks asked, standing up. He gestured at the screen. "The man confessed. Talking about spilling out blood like Kool-Aid."

"He doesn't fit the profile," Loshak said.

"Come on!" Spinks' eyebrows lurched up his forehead. "He sleeps on a couch. It's obvious the guy's a user. His alibi is that he was getting drunk at a dive bar where nobody saw him, for crying out loud!"

"Bevacqua's in his forties," Loshak said. But it was more than that. "Even if his lifestyle is a partial fit, you heard him chatting away in there. He's got social skills."

"You mean like confessing to murder?" Spinks said.

"He knows how to make conversation. Knows how to connect to someone else in the room. Doesn't shy away from eye contact. He's friendly, even. There's a warmth there, even if he might be a touch slow. Our killer's probably not the talkative sort. More withdrawn. Certainly the opposite of warm."

"So, because the guy's a little loquacious you're just going to let him go?" Spinks asked, an expression of supreme disbelief on his face.

Loshak glanced at the detectives. "I mean, I doubt they're just going to let him go."

Hwang leaned a broad shoulder against the wall and yawned. "Nah, we'll keep him for now. Keep him talking as long as we can. Personally, I doubt it leads anywhere, but we'll exhaust the lead before we move on from him. You can be certain of that."

Though Spinks seemed less than thrilled, Loshak was glad to hear it. They wouldn't need him for this part, and he had some sleep to catch up on.

The agent had just about made it to his rental when he heard the scuffing of shoes on the asphalt behind him. The smooth baritone that followed came as no surprise at all.

"You headed straight to bed?" Spinks said.

Loshak turned just as the reporter sidled up next to the sedan with what the agent took to be a hopeful look on his face. A streetlight flickered above the parking lot, reflected off the matte enamel on the car to their left.

"Yeah," Loshak said. "To be honest, I could really use the sleep. Been running on fumes for a few hours now."

Spinks' posture sagged right away, head tilting toward the ground for a beat.

"Damn. Sorry to hear that. I'm a little wired, I guess. I was all worked up, thinking we had this guy. I can't see sleeping for a while yet."

"No?"

"Don't think so, no." The reporter shrugged and stuck his hands in his pockets. "Want to grab something to eat?

Probably just drive-throughs open right now, but we could talk over the facts of the case a little. Wind down."

The idea that this had more to do with Spinks not wanting to go home to his wife's distant friendship than a lead not panning out surfaced in Loshak's mind. He rubbed a knuckle at the corner of his right eye, felt a piece of grit come loose and fall away. He wanted to say no. Wanted to race to his room, crank up the AC to full blast, and fall asleep so deeply he woke up confused about what state he was in or what year it was. Or both.

But when he looked into Spinks' face and saw how damn desperate the guy looked, he couldn't bring himself to say no.

CHAPTER 29

The Mac and Cheese Dog Loshak had ordered oozed greasy cheese sauce all over his hands as he bit into it. He held the little paper boat it came in under his chin to catch any spillage.

It wouldn't win any health food awards, and heartburn was almost a guarantee, but as far as late night fast food options went, it was at least a cut above Burger King and some of the others, in his estimation.

As Loshak chewed, he wiped the cheesy goop from his fingers onto a brown paper napkin. He glanced over at Spinks, who was tearing into his food. Loshak couldn't remember all the toppings listed on the hot dog monstrosity Spinks had chosen – mozzarella, bacon, and pineapple were the three he knew for certain, and he could see shoestring potatoes on top. Whatever else was on there, it sounded more like some kind of punishment than anything Loshak would willingly consume.

Judging by the way Spinks was mowing through his meal, Loshak would have expected the teal shirt he was wearing to suffer some collateral damage. Not so. In fact, Loshak couldn't detect so much as a crumb out of place. After every bite, the reporter meticulously wiped his mouth and hands as if he weren't about to pick the culprit up again and start the process over with the next bite. He'd already used a good three-quarters of the stack of napkins they'd been given. The dirties sat neatly folded in a pile

161

inside his cardboard hot dog tray.

"How's yours?" Spinks asked.

Loshak shrugged and popped a stray elbow noodle into his mouth.

"I never understood the whole gourmet hot dog thing," he said.

Ice rattled against the side of the cup Spinks held to his mouth. He took a long pull of sweet tea and then squinted at Loshak dubiously.

"You don't like hot dogs?"

"I don't like paying more than an entire pack of franks and a bag of buns for a single hot dog, no."

Spinks pointed at the mess in Loshak's paper boat.

"But what about the mac and cheese? You're not being fair."

"That's a symptom of a bigger problem. Why are we serving one food on top of another completely unrelated food? The two have nothing to do with one another. What's wrong with serving the hot dog and the macaroni and cheese separately?"

Spinks slurped more tea. Swallowing, he tipped the cup toward Loshak.

"Is this about me dragging you out after your bedtime?"

"What? No. I'm just saying, if you want a hot dog, eat a hot dog. If you want mac and cheese, eat mac and cheese."

"And I'm just saying, clock strikes midnight, and you turn ornery." The reporter used another napkin, folded it and added it to the pile. "Your mom never fixed you mac and cheese with franks cut up in it?"

Loshak chuckled. "I think the kids whose moms made that for supper were the ones my mom warned me not to play with. She'd roll over in her grave if she knew we were calling this stuff gourmet nowadays."

Spinks finished his Hot Dog of Cosmic Horror and dabbed imaginary smears from his face. When he was finished, he folded the napkin twice and tucked it into the cardboard tray with the rest.

He sighed, one hand on his stomach. "I could almost go for another, but I've got to save room for some humble pie."

"What's that now?"

Turning in his seat to face Loshak more squarely, Spinks propped an elbow up on the steering wheel. "I've always thought of myself as having an aptitude for reading people. A sort of natural compass for human nature. A proclivity, if you will."

Loshak finished off his deconstructed mac'n'cheese'n'frank. "Yeah?"

Spinks nodded.

"But tonight, well…" He pursed his lips, frowning a little. "I let my emotions get the better of me. Got me all stirred up inside, thinking about the Iverson girl. The Nicholson kids. It was almost like I *wanted* Larry the wino to be the killer so badly that I ignored all the evidence to the contrary and convinced myself it had to be him. Does that make sense?"

"Of course. Happens all the time, even to the best of us. Tunnel vision." Loshak wiped the last of the cheese goop from his fingertips. "There's a desperation to these serial cases. It can feel like we're working in the dark, grasping at straws most of the time. Some investigations go months without a lead. So when a real, live suspect finally falls into your lap, confession and all, the last thing you want to believe is that it's another dead end, that the real killer is still out there, maybe killing someone else."

Spinks exhaled loudly and hung his head.

"I hope we find him quick."

"Me too," Loshak agreed.

He finished scraping the last bits of mac and cheese from his tray with a plastic fork then set about collecting all of their trash.

It was a balmy night outside of the air-conditioned interior of the car. The air was so heavy with moisture, Loshak felt like he was half-swimming through it as he crossed the sidewalk to the garbage bin. He tossed the remnants of their meal and waded back to the car.

Spinks had his phone out when Loshak got back inside. The blue-white glow from the screen lit his face like he was a kid with a flashlight telling ghost stories.

"You wanna know something I don't get?" Spinks said.

"What's that?"

"Millennials."

Loshak closed his eyes. Nodded. He'd heard a rant or two about this group before, though if he was honest with himself, he had a hard time differentiating them from Generation X or really anyone under 50 or so. At some point, they'd all started to look like kids to him.

Spinks thumbed off his phone and stuck it in the cupholder. "They hate newspapers. They hate cars. They hate phone calls. They hate Applebees. Applebees! What the hell is wrong with Applebees?"

"Food sucks, for one thing," Loshak said. "Actually, I hate all the things you just named, so… Guess that makes me a millennial."

Spinks laughed.

"OK," the reporter said. "What about baseball?"

"Hate it."

"Golf?"

"To watch or to play? Actually, never mind. I hate it either way."

"Fabric softener?

"Scam."

"What about coupons?"

Loshak furrowed his brow. "Like saving money on stuff?"

"I mean cutting coupons out of a leaflet and saving 50 cents on something at the grocery store."

"Oh, lord no. Literally never done that in my life."

Spinks nodded. "OK. So far, you're a spot-on millennial, you even used the word 'literally' — although you used it in the right context. But here's a big one: Doritos?"

Loshak blinked.

"Those are actually good. Millennials hate Doritos?"

"Just the opposite, my friend. They love them. And that makes it official. You really are a 55-year-old millennial. Congratulations."

"53," Loshak said. "But you were close enough, I guess."

"OK, wait. Back up a second. How the hell is fabric softener a scam?"

"I've been washing my clothes for years without fabric softener. No difference."

Spinks raised an eyebrow, like maybe he didn't quite believe Loshak's claim.

"Try it without the next time you wash your clothes," Loshak said. "It's exactly the same."

"Yeah, but what about your fresh spring lavender scent?" Spinks shook his head and put the car in gear. "I'm not sure I want to live in a world where my shirts don't smell like a scented candle store."

Loshak shrugged. "Is a smell that lasts five minutes worth the extra thirty bucks a year, though? They're hard on the machines, too. Most laundromats don't even let you use them anymore."

"Guess we ought to call it a night," Spinks said, pulling out onto the street. "The millennial's getting cranky and railing against the accepted way of doing things."

Loshak smirked out at the darkened cityscape blurring past his window, thinking that a generation of people who challenged the societal norms based on their impracticality wouldn't be so bad. He could get on board with this millennial thing.

As they drove, Spinks told Loshak about a piece he'd been working on, the one he'd finished just before the serial killer story caught his eye.

"Police shooting of a 16-year-old kid. Had a sandwich in his hand when they shot him, wrapped in aluminum foil. Cop said he thought it was a gun."

"It's hard to wrap your head around, but there are some bad police out there," Loshak said.

"See, I thought the same thing at first. But once I let it stew for a while, I decided there had to be more to it. There are certainly bad cops, yeah," Spinks said. "But they can't all be bad. Probably not even most of them. That's what I believe, anyhow. And this particular incident wasn't a race thing if that's what you're thinking. Latino cop and Latino kid. Sometimes police abuse their power in awful ways, but sometimes it's something else."

"Like what?"

Spinks tapped the side of his head. "A fault in the human brain, more or less. Has to do with rapid cognition. I first read about it in this Malcolm Gladwell book a few years ago."

"Oh yeah. I think I read one of those," Loshak said. "*Outliers*, maybe."

"Well, rapid cognition is basically the concept of all the thinking we do without thinking. This stream of observations and predictions that happen in our subconscious minds. They affect everything we do. The little snap judgments our right brains make. They happen in a blink, just like that."

Spinks snapped his fingers.

"We read people's minds all the time by looking into their eyes, interpreting the expressions on their faces. And we use these things to judge whether they're being sincere or sarcastic, genuine or misleading. We depend on this flow of information constantly without ever really thinking about it."

Loshak bobbed his head up and down. He had to make those gut feeling judgment calls all the time in his work.

"But in moments of intense crisis, the ability leaves us," the reporter continued. "Panic kind of short circuits our brains, whittles our focus down to the immediate threat or anxiety, so much so that scientists say it's like a form of temporary autism. Our ability to filter and process all the stimulus around us is severely impeded, which is textbook autism, you know? In moments of panic, we simply can no longer think the way we normally do."

Spinks reached for his phone and held it up as if it were a courtroom exhibit.

"It leaves a panicked individual unable to perform routine tasks. Like dialing 9-1-1. Pretty simple right? But a lot of people can't remember how to do it in moments of crisis. They misdial. Crazy as that seems. Three digits become too much to deal with. Overwhelms them."

The phone went back into the cupholder, and Spinks went on.

"So this cop saw this kid walking along in the dark. And he misread something. Got spooked somehow. And his mind jumped to the serial rapist who's been terrorizing Dade County. The kid looked just like the sketch we have on that one, in the dark, at least. And the next thing the officer knew, his brain was short-circuiting, right? And he didn't see a sandwich in the kid's hand. He saw a gun. A gun raising to point at him. It's a real phenomenon when we're in that state of temporary autism. Just like that inability to dial 9-1-1."

The car curled into the hotel parking lot now. Spinks pulled up to the lobby, put the car in park, but left the engine running.

"Of course, like I said. Some of 'em are just bad cops. And sometimes it's hard to tell the difference, but... I guess what got me thinking about it was my reaction to Bevacqua earlier. Tensions were running high, and I wanted so badly to catch the guy that I stopped using my eyes and ears to really look at what I was seeing. To hear all the ways he didn't fit. Some animal part in me just wanted to get it all over with. It was instinct more than anything. Dumb instinct."

Loshak shifted in his seat. It made sense, of course. But it also made him uncomfortable. To be in a position where he often operated on his gut feeling, and to wonder if someday it would lead him astray. He didn't like that.

"What do you think?" Spinks asked. "You've been in some hairy situations. Shoot first, ask questions later kind of scenarios. Haven't you?"

Running a hand through his hair, Loshak shook his head.

"I mean, I guess so. But I think I've always wanted to believe that I keep my head when the shit hits the fan. Now that I think about it, though, how could I have? When the adrenaline kicks in, when you're fully in fight-or-flight mode, it is all instinct and impulse. It's like flipping a switch to a different part of your brain. The cold-blooded part that has to be ready to strike, ready to pull the trigger if it comes to that."

Loshak turned and looked Spinks in the eye.

"It's kind of scary to think about it that way. To worry that someday the switch might get flipped, and it'll all go wrong."

"Makes sense," Spinks said. "For a guy like you, that's probably your worst nightmare."

Loshak lifted his eyebrow. "A guy like me?"

"You're all up here," Spinks said, tapping his head. "Cerebral. Thinker. Reasoner. The thought of the tool you base all your actions on someday betraying you has to be terrifying. Cause what do you do once it's gone?"

They were silent for a moment, the heaviness of that

potential wrong reaction hanging in the air, dampening the atmosphere of the car until it was something muggy and dark. Sapping the little energy he'd had before eating until he was down to nothing. Loshak rubbed at gritty eyes and tried to hold back a yawn.

Spinks startled him by clapping him on the shoulder.

"Hey, thanks for coming out with me. I appreciate it. Now go get some sleep."

Loshak undid his seatbelt and climbed out of the car, telling Spinks goodnight somewhere in there.

His eyelids were heavier now than they'd been in years. He glided up to his room and was asleep less than a minute after his body hit the bed.

CHAPTER 30

It took a long time to settle down after the kill in the parking lot. A long time.

The gory movie still played in his head. The close-up shot of the knife skewering the soft place in the otherwise heavily muscled throat. Gashing it wide. The blood glugging out in weird spirals. Thick rivulets of red. Separate streams that seemed to tangle over each other like a braid.

The man in black drove for hours while the images played in his head. Circled the city like a vulture. Breathing smoke through the filtered tips of his Winstons.

He savored it. The perpetual motion. That tangy tobacco taste, that little electric sizzle where the nicotine goodness touched the lining of his lip. These sensations had become his dearest companions in this world, in this life.

Maybe these were his only real connections to anyone or anything outside of himself that lasted. Momentum and the smokes would never leave him, would always treat him right, no matter what he said or did.

So long as big tobacco existed to sell cancer by the carton, he'd have at least one friend, wouldn't he? He wished that were a comforting thought. Stubbed a butt out in the ashtray. Lit another one. The lighter's flame flickered orange reflections in the sheen of his greasy face, fresh smoke twirling into his chest.

The coke, unlike the cigarettes, could be such a harsh mistress. Not to be trusted, that one. It came on hot and fast, flushed a wet warmth into his limbs, made him feel so impossibly confident for a time, like a rock star and a professional athlete and a Norse god all rolled into one.

But it always left him just as quickly. Always fled the same way. Abandoned him. A quick fade from euphoria that ended in a crash.

An imploding building. A collapsing star. A tablecloth ripped off the table and all the dishes exploding into useless shards.

He wanted only to believe all the lies the cocaine told him, all the grand things it made him feel. And he did while it lasted. But all those narcissistic fantasies dissolved, deflated like an untied balloon whooshing around the room, all those harsh realities rushing in to take their place.

An ugly world.

An ugly self.

It made him feel empty. Worse than before.

That's where he was now. Abandoned by his one true love. Dumped and forgotten. An itchy stick man, driving and scratching and chain-smoking his Winstons. Reeking like ammonia and old French fry grease. Skin slicked with perspiration, beads of it standing out on his forehead and along his jawline. Body somehow too hot and too cold at the same time. Eyes so sore they felt like metal shavings had been sprinkled in them and rubbed in pretty good with knuckles.

He no longer saw the city as he drove. No longer took in either the sights or sounds. The buildings. The pedestrians. The palm trees. The haze hanging over the skyline like the humidity had congealed into an opaque steam around them. He saw none of these.

Everything outside was a blur. Featureless and distant.

His camera pointed inside. Exclusively. Obsessively.

He observed himself. Watched the little tremors shiver in his arms and shimmy his shoulders now and then. Watched the hand move the cigarette to the cracked window to flick away ashes.

But he kept moving, plunging through the murk outside. Kept swimming forward like a shark fighting against the current. Gritting his teeth. Pensive. Waiting. Waiting for the scent of blood to find its way to his nostrils like it always eventually did.

The next house.

The next victim.

They'd present themselves in time. And he would be ready.

He drove. Clenched his teeth and drove.

The sun rose to vanquish the night, ascended to its peak, and started its way down. The day burned up and started to fade, and he never stopped driving. Never stopped moving all the while.

Eventually he would sleep. Maybe. Could be today. Could be three days from now. Depended on how things went after the dark, if and when he slipped into the next house, came away with his next round of spoils, his next haul loaded up in a silverware drawer. So many variables.

What would he get tonight? Who would he get tonight? The lucky winner, right?

Some poor soul would wake up in the dead of the night with nine inches of hard steel ripping their fucking neck open so wide you could gently nestle a grapefruit in the cavity without so much as touching the open flaps. They'd wake up just long enough to die, pretty much. He smiled a little when he thought about it like that.

The irony. Sucks to be them, right?

But this was the way of the fucking world. The sheep existed for the wolves to slaughter and feast upon.

Too bad.

Fuck you.

It was nature. The order of the natural world. No other way to it.

All you motherfuckers live your whole lives long in your fuckin' pens, and you think that little swath of grass surrounded by posts and railing is the whole fucking world. That you'll be safe so long as you stay with the herd.

Well, I've got news, and it ain't good. It's right here at the tip of my fucking knife, and I can carve the breaking story into your fucking skin if you like. Scrawl the headline in bright red just under your flabby chin.

He smiled harder. And for just this moment he didn't feel the itch crawling over his scalp. Felt no pain at all. Just that glow like his mistress had come back to numb him a while a longer.

Fucking housecats, all of you. Neutered and declawed. Too dumb to see that you're fucking trapped in some suburban home.

Well, the big dog is strutting into your neighborhood tonight, nuts intact. Coming to show you what the real world is like. What it's always been like.

The big animals eat the little ones. Always have, always will.

The car accelerated at the touch of his foot. Growled a little as he weaved in and out of lanes. Hurtling ever forward. Agitated. Building speed slowly but surely.

And sometimes he felt like there was a hole where his heart should be. A chasm. A vacancy.

Maybe there was some scrap of something left. Some caved in piece of meat. Blackened. A pitiful withered thing.

But something key had been removed, he was certain of that. Some fundamental piece of what being human must entail, what humanity must mean. Empathy or compassion or some such thing. Something essential was missing. Gone.

Beaten out of him. Ripped out by rough hands.

And now he was something else. Something damaged beyond repair. Something new. Something wild and violent and free. Something savage.

Untamed.

Ferocious.

A rabid fucking dog leaping straight for your goddamn jugular.

And it made sense, he thought. It made perfect sense. Somewhere way down deep in his gut, it felt right. The same way the cocaine felt right.

Because this was what happened when the world abused someone long enough. Hurt him every which way for all those years. Belittled him. Defiled him. Bruised him inside and out.

This was what fucking happened.

There would be no fixing it. Not ever. No doctors to mend the damage done. No psychiatrist who could erase the scars seared into his psyche.

He was an animal the world had backed into a corner. A wounded creature. Frightened and small and fighting to stay alive, fighting to exist at all. So what else could he do but bare his fangs? What else could he do but lash out?

Attack. Attack. Attack.

Strike out at the world who had fucked him this way. Strike out at the society who had let it happen, watched it happen. Strike out at the people, any people.

All the people.

Crawl into their windows and savage them where they slept.

Crawl into their windows to steal their breath.

Take what he wanted for once. And wasn't it all the better to take it by force? Express all his hurt and anger through the sharp edge of his blade? Make his point in red so bright that it couldn't be ignored?

Yes. Much better, thank you very much. So much better.

There came a breaking point for any man, he thought, no matter how meek he may be. A point where slitting throats was the only thing that made any goddamn sense at all. A point of desperation where it became the only option, the only avenue to self-respect.

So he lashed out. And he fought back. And he liked it. And he thought it good.

Developed a taste for it like violence was a gourmet feast.

And what else could a wounded animal do? It was a kind of destiny, he thought. The path of destruction he left was the only path he could see available to him. The only way to go.

And he knew in that blackened remnant of a heart where this path would lead. He would lash out again and again and again. He would carve a bloody trail through the suburbs by night until someone came along and put this wounded animal down for good.

CHAPTER 31

Loshak's phone woke him up again the next morning. He answered, wondering if everyone just waited until they knew he was asleep to call.

"Mary Iverson is awake," Spinks said. "The girl from the other night, the one our killer bludgeoned."

Loshak sat up. "She's talking?"

"No." Spinks hesitated. "Well, I mean, kind of."

Loshak scrubbed at his eyes while he tried to get some meaning out of that. He couldn't. He was running on too little sleep and too little coffee, and frankly, it sounded like nonsense.

"What?" he asked.

"She's communicating some. Not talking exactly, but…" Spinks let the thought trail off.

Loshak was out of bed now, feet moving him across the carpet without him telling them to. He peeled open the part in the curtains a tiny crack and a blade of blinding sunlight cut into the room. He recoiled from the brightness like he was a vampire.

His eyes burned. Watered. Shrank away from the piercing light that seemed to stab them.

He backpedaled a few steps, somehow winding up in something of a karate stance, his shoulders heaving a little.

He didn't burst into flames, however, so he figured he might as well get on with the day.

"I'll be down there in fifteen minutes," he said.

*   *   *

The atmosphere in the girl's hospital room was strange. Quiet. The hanging plastic slats over the window were pulled closed and flat. According to the mother, the sunlight hurt Mary's eyes and head. So the shade was deep, the room stuck in the in-between hour of dusk.

To Loshak, it felt shrouded. Everyone there — the parents, Detective Renaud, even the nurses when they came in — spoke in low, soothing tones. Like anything louder than a whisper would spook the girl.

And maybe it would have. She didn't seem right. Frail and strange. Like she wasn't all the way there. Every time she blinked, there was a weird hitch as though the lashes were stuck together. It made her left eye open and close slower than the right.

Loshak expected to feel a sort of revulsion to seeing another teenage girl lying in a hospital bed, a fear or apprehension or even a flashback to Shelly, but the comparison wasn't there. The energy in the room was completely different.

Mary Iverson was sitting up in bed, frail but not skeletal. Damaged, but not dying. And the smell wasn't right. That rotting sweetness that air fresheners and antiseptic couldn't cover. The room was quiet, but it wasn't sepulchral. This was a girl who was going to keep on living. Maybe the blink would never go back to normal. Maybe she'd have trouble talking for the rest of her life, but she would *have* a rest of her life.

While Loshak watched, the girl's mother took a little dry erase board from the rolling table and set it on Mary's lap, then found the marker and put it in the girl's hand,

179

closing her fingers around it. Rather than holding it between her middle and ring finger the way most people wrote, the girl kept it clutched in her whole fist, like a toddler with a crayon.

"Mary," Detective Renaud began, his voice low. He waited for her eyes to focus on him before continuing. "We'd like to ask you a few questions about the guy who hurt you. Would that be all right?"

That weird, out-of-sync blink. Then another. Finally, Mary nodded.

"Thanks, Mary," Renaud said. Even his smile was slow. Loshak found himself thinking, *No sudden movements.* "Did the guy have dark or light hair?"

Mary took a deep breath and started to write, concentrating hard. The marker squeaked on the board as she produced big, childish letters. Sloppy and capital.

DARK, the board said.

"What about his eyes?" Renaud asked.

She tapped the board.

DARK.

"His eyes and hair were both dark?"

She nodded.

"Good," Renaud said. "Great. Could you tell his… ethnicity?"

WHITE, she wrote.

Renaud jotted this in a little notepad. "Was he tall? Short?"

After several slow, strange blinks, Mary shook her head, one shoulder twitching in a shrug.

"Don't remember?"

Mary shrugged again, but Loshak thought it was more

likely that she meant she hadn't been able to tell. She'd been strangled in her bed, lying down. How did you read the height of someone leaning over you?

"That's okay," Renaud said. "Can you tell me whether he was fat or thin?"

She erased her board, then wrote, *THIN*.

"Was he young like you—" the detective asked, gesturing at her, then pointing at his chest "—or old like me?"

This drew a hint of a smile from her.

YOUNG. Then she frowned. After a few seconds' thought, she added a question mark.

Loshak stepped in closer. "Do you think he was closer to your age or your parents'?"

MYNE? She blinked, looking at the board, then erased the Y and wrote in an I.

Not being a neurologist, Loshak couldn't say for sure, but he thought it was a good sign that she was recognizing mistakes and correcting them. Maybe it meant the damage wasn't permanent.

"Is there anything else you can remember about this guy?" Renaud asked.

Mary didn't have to think about this one. She began writing immediately.

SMELLY! EGGS + B.O.

"Did he have any scars or birthmarks?" the detective asked. "Anything you saw that would make you go 'That's him!' if you ever saw him again."

Her eyes went wide. She scribbled at the whiteboard, but not words. For a moment, Loshak wondered if the questioning had taxed her too much and she was losing her ability to write coherently as she got tired.

But slowly, the marks started to coalesce into something. A cross. Mary stopped to think, her eyes blinking that strange off-beat shuffle, then she added a second line below the crossbar. Under that she drew a figure eight lying on its side.

Loshak's mind jumped ahead. "It's a tattoo, isn't it?"

Mary nodded, her eyes shining with appreciation for being understood.

"Where was it?" he asked. When she started to erase her whiteboard again, Loshak said, "Can you show us?"

She lifted her finger and pointed at her forearm, just below the crook of her elbow.

CHAPTER 32

"It's called a Leviathan Cross," Spinks said, turning his phone's screen to face Loshak. The symbol on the screen looked nearly identical to Mary Iverson's drawing, apparently the same symbol inked into the killer's skin.

As a member of the press, Spinks hadn't been allowed into the girl's hospital room, but he'd been waiting outside for Loshak to fill him in. Now they walked and talked, moving down the hospital halls at a brisk pace, Spinks scrolling down on his phone to read more about the strange symbol.

"Also known as the Brimstone Cross if you're in China," the reporter continued. "It was adopted by Anton LaVey in the sixties as the symbol of Satanism, his Church of Satan branch of that, anyway, and now it's on their bible, but apparently the Knights Templar created it long ago. Also, turns out it's the symbol of sulfur. Fun fact."

They turned down a hallway, a pair of elevators waiting at the end.

"Huh," Loshak said.

"What?"

"The girl said our killer smelled like rotten eggs," Loshak said. "Pretty strong in her memory, given how excited she got when she wrote it. That's how a lot of people describe the smell of hydrogen sulfide."

Spinks' eyes went wide, but his smile gave away his amusement. "You know who else smells like sulfur?

183

Supposedly, I mean."

They stopped at the elevators.

"Who?"

"Satan."

Loshak chuckled and hit the Down button. "I don't think he's our guy. She didn't mention a pitchfork or a tail or anything. No cloven hooves. Not even so much as a goatee."

Spinks chuckled at that. Loshak went on.

"It's not the first time we've seen something like this, of course. Some occult or otherwise creepy symbols or messages linked to serial murder cases. Whether it was Richard Ramirez drawing a pentagram on a woman's leg with lipstick, or even the Manson family doing bloody finger paintings about piggies and Helter Skelter on the walls of the LaBianca house, there's a long history of this kind of crap. And it's all an act. The sickos get off on it, I suppose. Scaring everyone. Getting under the public's skin, capturing their imagination with all of this darkness. It's part of their fantasy, the infamy of it all. Maybe some of them even start to believe it a little. Makes them feel powerful, you know?"

Loshak shook his head.

"But for the most part, it's pure histrionics. Hell, Ramirez scrawled another pentagram on the palm of his hand to flash to the press photographers in court. Yelled 'Hail Satan!' during his jury selection. At that point, it's a straight-up publicity stunt, you know? A serial killer photo-op. And the media ate it up, of course. Splashed his mug on the front page just the way he wanted them to."

The elevator door retracted into the wall before them,

and they stepped into the little chamber, waiting a moment to be whisked away.

"No," Loshak said again. "We're looking for an ordinary — albeit smelly — psychopath."

CHAPTER 33

With the tattoo to go on, it was time to compile mugshots of possible suspects. Loshak and Spinks met Detectives Renaud and Hwang at the Tamarac station to help go through the inmate database.

In addition to the standard vital statistics, current and former inmates were searchable by their tattoos and identifying marks that had been logged at the time of processing. These were updated whenever an offender was arrested again.

The whole endeavor depended on their killer having been arrested before, but Loshak felt good about that. A likelihood of previous drug and impulse-related offenses fit the profile. It would be a big surprise, bordering on a miracle, if a guy this chaotic hadn't gotten popped at some point, be it for shoplifting, assault, or indecent exposure. Take your pick, Loshak thought.

Searching the database for notes relating to tattoos of strange symbols left them with hundreds of results. Not exactly practical for four people to wade through while they had a killer walking the streets.

"Filter it down to anybody arrested in the Dade County area in the last two years," Loshak suggested.

Renaud entered the dates and county into the appropriate boxes.

"From seven hundred down to fifty-nine," the mousy detective announced.

"Yeah, but how many of these guys are current guests?" Hwang asked, leaning over her partner's shoulder to scan the results.

Renaud deselected the box for current inmates. "That leaves us with thirty-one possible matches."

While Hwang updated Chief Moretti so their new leads could be entered into the task force database, the rest of them arranged the mugshots into a binder. They would show these to the girl and see if she recognized anyone.

Loshak felt the familiar anticipation building in his chest while they worked, a feeling like a knot pulling tight or handcuffs ratcheting shut. They were closing in.

*   *   *

It was just after noon when Loshak and the detectives made it back to the hospital. A small, round nurse in blue scrubs informed them that Mary Iverson was asleep. They were forced to mill around the waiting room drinking shitty hospital coffee until she woke up.

Whether from the coffee or the excitement, Loshak could hardly sit still. He kept shaking his leg and checking his watch every two minutes. They were close, he knew it, and sitting around, marking time felt ridiculous, bordering on insane. But the kid had been strangled nearly to death and smashed in the head so hard that it fractured her skull. The least they could do was let her get a few more minutes' sleep while her body tried to put itself back together.

While they waited, Renaud tried to draw him into conversation. Loshak didn't have much to offer in return. He was thinking about the next steps. Where they would go from here if Mary identified their killer in the binder, or what they would do if she didn't recognize any of the mugshots.

Renaud seemed determined to get Loshak to talk about something. He brought up the weather in Florida — "Crazy how they call it the Sunshine State, but yet every day around four we get those showers." — sports — "I never much cared for football myself. Soccer, now, that's an athlete's game. Those guys just run for 90 minutes at a time. That's endurance, my friend. Not this football crap where they play for 3 seconds and spend damn near a minute getting around for the next snap." — and the task force database — "You got the notifications on? Mine went off last night at three a.m. I'd just got home from talking to our bus station buddy, filling out all the damn paperwork involved in that goose chase, laid down, and relaxed when it started dinging. I had half a mind to shut it off right then."

Loshak thought it was likely that this was the mousy detective's version of shaking his leg or pacing. He wished Spinks was there to act as a buffer, intercept some of Renaud's conversation attempts, but Spinks had taken off to get some "real work" done since he wouldn't be allowed into the hospital room anyway.

Finally, the little nurse reappeared. "Y'all can go in now."

They stepped into the hushed dusk of Mary's room. Her mother wasn't there this time, but a heavy middle-aged man had taken Mom's place. The dad, Loshak guessed. Unlike Mom, Dad didn't get out of the way when they eased up to Mary's bedside. Instead, he puffed up a little, hovering protectively over his daughter. Loshak stayed back a bit, letting the guy know with his body language that he wasn't a threat. Whether Renaud picked up on the maneuver consciously or subconsciously Loshak couldn't tell, but the detective hung back as well.

"Mary, based on the description you gave us, we were able to put together a book of mugshots for you to look at." Loshak had to stretch a little to get the book into her reach.

Before she could take it, the dad snatched the binder from him and propped it on his daughter's lap with excessive care. Like he was afraid she would shatter if he moved too fast.

"If you could take a look at them and let us know what you think, it'd be really helpful," Loshak said. "And if none of them look right, you'll still be helping us narrow it down."

Mary opened the binder and studied the photos, curiosity and determination etched in the lines of her face. It made her look older, Loshak thought. Like the woman she would become instead of the teenager she was.

She flipped to the second page. Right away, her eyes went wide, and she gasped. She tapped the fourth photo in the third row, *tat tat tat*. Emphatic. No hesitation in her movements. No doubt at all.

Loshak leaned closer, ignoring the father this time, and stared into the dark eyes of the murderer. Printed below the mugshot was his information.

His name was Edward Zakarian.

CHAPTER 34

The cocaine and the money were gone. That thought kept slamming to the surface of the man in black's brain as he drove around. Gone. No more. None left.

The faintest of tremors rattled the palms of his hands against the steering wheel. Sweat beaded on his temples, in the hairs on his upper lip, wet his shirt under his pits.

It wasn't good. He was coming down the rest of the way. Bad time for it, too. He'd heard his name on the radio earlier — the fucking cops knew his name — and now he couldn't calm down. He was amped out of control, thinking about how they were probably plastering his picture all over TV, wanted posters in supermarkets and post offices, the whole nine yards.

And all because of that girl, that moment of weakness. This was what he got for being a pussy, for letting her live, and he could never take it back. It replayed in his head as he cruised the city, that moment of panic, the lamp cord slipping through his fingers, him running scared. His weakness was being punished.

But he'd undone that some, hadn't he? Took down 275 pounds of steroid-infested wrestler meat. In his mind, the man in black saw again the tangled streams of blood coiling out of his neck like dark liquid snakes. That had to count for something. As long as he was strong, he couldn't lose. Couldn't be caught.

His stomach growled. The coke usually kept it quiet,

suppressed his appetite while he filled his body with alcohol, but now he was starving. Empty. Itching and lonely and cold.

He fumbled in his pocket and came up with three dollars and a handful of coins. Just enough to get a couple microwave burritos at the gas station tonight, maybe. If he couldn't score between now and then, which seemed iffy at the moment.

In the dash, the gas gauge showed a needle approaching E. Fuck that. You never saw the guy in the movies pumping gas. Nobody ever saw the man in black pumping gas, either, because he didn't. If this car ran out, he'd just steal another one. No fuckin' problem there.

But he needed something else in the meantime, didn't he? Yes, yes. Something to take the edge away, to take the dreams away, the pictures of the girl that came to him over and over. Waking nightmares. Violent pictures that plagued his thoughts, emasculated him, washed those feelings of failure over him again and again.

Those needed killing. Needed to be drowned out with drugs or strong drink.

He licked his lips, filled with a lust for substances to abuse. And he gripped the steering wheel a little harder, fingers twisting around the smooth plastic ring like he could strangle that and solve all of his problems right here and now.

He needed something to distort reality to such a degree that it could be tolerated again, for a little while, anyway. Something strong. Potent. Something to knock his brain into a stupor for a nice long stretch.

Shit yeah, that sounded good. Sounded good as hell.

If he could just make it until dark, shut his higher brain down until the sun disappeared and the night finally rolled around, he knew he'd be fine. The night always had a way of sharpening his focus, calming him, melting the anxiety away, waking him up.

He'd become nocturnal over time, he realized. A solitary creature who walked the night, kept to the shadows, more comfortable in the places where the light could never reach. So he just needed to bridge that little gap between now and then, that was all.

OK, so he'd come to a decision. He had to kill the next four to six hours. And he required a strong substance to assist in that process. A simple enough task, apart from his lack of funds.

He would need to get creative. His tongue flicked over his lips again, and he knew what to do.

CHAPTER 35

Loshak stepped onto Jan's porch, glad to see there were no signs of dead rodents on her welcome mat, and rang the bell.

He was here on a personal call, of course, checking in while he had a minute, but that didn't stop the details of the case from buzzing around in his head. He was much too excited to slow that hornet's nest in his skull down even a little.

Zakarian's mugshot had gone out to the press not long ago – plus a few bonus photos from a dormant Myspace account, dated but still potentially useful. His name had gone out over the radio already, and Loshak had a hunch that the tips would roll in quickly once the local TV news plastered the photos everywhere.

He could see those dark eyes in his mind now. Dead eyes that stood out in every photo, even when he smiled. Shadowy pits more than anything. Other than that feature Loshak thought Edward Zakarian looked like a normal, if scrawny, 20-something scraping by in life. The kid was a metalhead from the looks of it, perpetually sporting tattered jeans and t-shirts with the sleeves cut off, almost every stitch of it black.

Loshak's mind drifted back to the here and now, focused on the task ahead of him – checking in on his ex-wife. He squared his shoulders at Jan's door, folded his hands in front of his waist.

Several seconds passed, however, with no flutter of life beyond the steel rectangle between him and her place. What the hell?

He stood on tiptoes to peer over the bushes. Jan's little Escape was in the carport. She must be here. He reached for the doorbell again, but the door opened before his finger got there.

The version of Jan that took shape in the doorway seemed frail. Stooped and delicate. Her eyes were puffy and wet, her lips quivering although she had them pressed into a thin line.

All thoughts of the case fled Loshak's mind at once.

"What the hell?" He followed her inside, a low-grade panic churning in his gut. "Jan, what's wrong?"

"I'm leaving," she snapped, and Loshak realized she had a wadded-up pair of jeans in her fist. Her voice was choked with phlegm. "Moving. Fuck this place. And fuck him."

"What happened?"

"Roxie." The dog's name did it. A sob interrupted whatever she meant to say next. Tears streaked down her cheeks. "That bastard left her head on the step."

It was like getting punched in the gut. Loshak's brain was nothing but blank space. He stepped toward his ex-wife, touching her arm, trying to impart some kind of physical comfort to make up for not knowing what to say, but Jan jerked away from him.

Loshak pulled his hand back stupidly. Still nothing came to mind that he could say.

"He has an alibi," she growled, the bundle of denim still clutched in her fist. "Of course he does. I called it in — right after I found her, I called the cops — but he flew out to Mexico last night. He'll be gone for two weeks. They even confirmed the flight records, so there's nothing to be done. He wins. I'll move. And I hope a hurricane blows this fucking house down on his head."

"Don't go," he said, aware that he sounded dazed, foolish. He cleared his throat. "You've got to stay and fight this asshole, Jan. We can beat him."

"Don't you get it?" she shrieked. "Roxie's dead! He won."

"No. We know he did it. We can charge him with—"

"I'm moving, Vick. End of discussion. I know you meant well when you talked to him…"

But you got my dog killed, Loshak finished for her.

Jan's fists clenched, then her shoulders slumped, all the fight draining out of her at once.

"Look, if you want to help, you can bury her for me. There's a garbage bag on the patio." New tears poured out as she said this. She reached up to swipe them away, dragging the wad of jeans across her face. She sniffed hard. "I know I should be the one to do it, but I can't. I just can't."

*   *   *

The shovel chopped into the grass, levering it aside to reveal a scoop of sandy dirt. Then little wedges of the earth slid out of the ground like strange slices cut out of a pie. Or like those fancy quenelles chefs had sometimes presented on reality TV shows Loshak had seen. He flung the loose stuff into a ragged pile along the lip of the hole and struck deeper into the next layer of soil.

The shock was fading as he performed this manual labor, and anger was taking its place, welling up like water filling a glass. Loshak couldn't believe that piece of shit Seidel.

How could he put Jan through this? A woman who lost her daughter and never really recovered. Who lost her husband as well, he supposed, to his own helpless grief. So this asshole takes her only companion, an innocent fucking dog, a tiny creature who never did anything to anyone. He brutalized it, decapitated it, and for what? For the right to charge some fucking extra rent? It was psychotic.

In his mind, Loshak could see Jan stepping out onto the porch to call the pup back inside. Seeing the head — just the head — lying there, bleeding. Maybe looking up at her. Christ only knew where the rest of the dog even was!

The words cut off in his head. Washed out by a surge of feelings. Rage like he hadn't felt in years. Something raw and red he didn't think he'd be able to contain for long.

The heat built up in his skull, a roiling angry fever. The shovel bit into the ground with greater and greater force, the sound swelling. Louder. More percussive. More solid.

And soon the only things that were real were the beat of that shovel cutting into the earth and that red tide swelling to overwhelm him.

A thought snapped into his head with great force. It wasn't just how could anybody do that to anyone. It wasn't an abstraction to ponder at arm's length like one of his cases. This one was very, very personal. It was how could someone do that *to Jan*. To his wife.

His arms shook with the fury boiling just under his skin. He couldn't hold the red tide back any longer. It gushed over him, lurching and violent. And he moved now without thought, crossed to the landlord's side of the duplex, and swung the shovel like a baseball bat at a rear window leading into the kitchen.

Glass shattered and sprayed. His chest heaved. Spit sprayed between his teeth.

And just like that, the red tide reached its highest point and rolled back, its power fleeing him over the course of a few seconds. Emptying him out.

He took a few breaths. Let the shovel fall to his side. Let gravity pull his shoulders into a stoop.

Then it was over, and he was tired, and all that was broken was a window. He looked at the cracked places in the glass. Found no satisfaction there. It had been a worthless gesture, an old man lashing out at something inanimate because he'd lost yet another fight.

He let his daughter die, let his wife suffer alone, goaded her landlord into killing the dog… What was a broken window compared to that?

Then the pain hit. Bright and stabbing, deep in his hands and wrists. For a second, the pain was so intense that he checked to see if he'd somehow cut himself on the broken glass.

But no. Not a scratch. He was just a weak old man who couldn't even break a window without suffering a bout of arthritis.

CHAPTER 36

As he pushed through the convenience store door, the man in black pulled the trucker hat down low so it covered his eyebrows and blocked out a good chunk of his field of vision. The hat was a crushed mesh thing he'd peeled off the floor behind the passenger's seat, and it said, "My Wife is on the Warpath Again," in bold blue letters. The kind of thing that someone probably won at a county fair in 1991 and stored safely on the floor of their car for decades at a time, perhaps worn ironically once or twice along the way.

The curled brim of the thing rode so low on his forehead that it butted up against the big Kim Jong-il sunglasses he'd dug out of the glove box. He was pretty sure they were women's shades, complete with a gold accent at the joint of the frames, and he cared not at all. Fuck it. The oversized lenses covered about half his face, and that suited him just fine.

The glass door swung shut behind him, and he strolled in like he owned the place. Shoulders back. Chest puffed out. Arms spread out at his sides like he was a damn superhero or something. He'd learned that confidence was the key to shoplifting. The confidence to do it without flinching, to look natural while behaving with brazen abandon. Always better to look strong and secure, even cocky, in this kind of situation, he thought.

Mammalian eyes looked for weakness out of habit, probed for fear and insecurity, primal instincts bred into us for countless generations. Meekness stood out like an erection in sweatpants, drawing instant scrutiny and attention. But arrogant assholes always looked natural, always looked like they belonged wherever they were. They were practically invisible that way.

He strutted like a rooster past a row of candy bars, a little tempted to pocket something with peanuts in it, before pulling up short in front of the wall of coolers lining the back of the place.

He walked down the row in slow motion, looking the six-packs up and down, pawing at his chin, looking for all the world like he just couldn't find what he was looking for, or hoping that's how he came off in any case.

Again, the beer was tempting. He could maybe get a 40 in his jeans if he really wanted, smuggle it out that way, but no.

Beer and candy wouldn't fill the emptiness, not the kind of gaping abyss he wanted to fill. He needed something stronger, something that could take him far away from here quickly and completely.

He snuck a peek at the cashier, a middle-aged man with thick black stubble that stretched from his cheekbones all the way down the length of his neck. Almost looked more like fur than human facial hair. The guy seemed busy with a customer, oblivious, turning away, fishing for some off-brand of cigarettes in the rows of packs filling a wall dispenser behind the counter.

The man in black made his move. Ducked into the aisle full of cleaning products. Slipped a can of duster into the waistband of his pants, the aluminum cold against his fish-white belly.

199

He glided back to the beer cooler and worked his way down the row of glass doors the way he'd come, not so slowly this time, eyes still dancing over the varieties of beer. He tried to express agitation in his movements. Frustration. Disbelief. They didn't have his brand of beer, damn it, he said with a tossing of his hands followed by a shrug.

After a sigh, he strutted out, puffing his chest up bigger than before. His body language told anyone happening to glance his way: *Fear not, no weakness here, just a big-dicked individual passing through with total confidence.*

He watched the clerk and customers at the counter out of the corner of his eye. None of them so much as blinked in his direction.

Damn, he was good.

The man in black pushed open the door and stepped away from the building.

CHAPTER 37

By the time Loshak made it back to the motel, the worst of the rage seemed to have passed. He was dirty and sweaty from digging a dog grave in subtropical temperatures, and he just wanted a shower and to lie down.

He shucked out of his clothes on the way to the bathroom, the air conditioning raising goose bumps when it connected with the sweat. A hot shower. The water pressure in this place was shit, and the so-called "massaging action" promised by the showerhead was laughable at best, but a hot shower was a hot shower. It would ease some of the tension in his back and shoulders, work out some of the stiffness from the manual labor. He'd probably be feeling it tomorrow, though.

But when he stepped onto the cold tile and flipped on the bathroom light, movement caught his eye.

It was the mirror, and once he saw it, he couldn't stop seeing it. Graying hair, soft flesh along a jaw that used to be sharp like a razor. He locked eyes with himself. The rage swelled again, coming to a boil almost immediately. The image of the garbage bag was so clear that he could almost feel himself holding it again, the plastic pulled taut by the weight of Roxie's head.

He heard Jan crying. Saw her wiping her eyes with those wadded-up jeans.

All of it exploded inside him. He drove his fist into the motel mirror. With the half-crunch, half-tinkling of shattered glass, his reflection cracked, then fell apart.

Blood welled up right away, weeping from his knuckles. And somehow, the back of his hand, too.

And the most aggressive part of him was somehow pleased, somehow appeased by the letting of blood. Felt it right in a primal way that made him clench his teeth and bare them a little in something akin to a smile.

Good. If he had to hurt, there should at least be some blood to show for it.

He watched it slip down his fingers and wrist, watched as the red dripped into the sink and onto the counter. But this didn't change anything, either. Didn't fix anything. Didn't even relieve the anger. That was still there, boiling, just waiting to bubble over again.

Just another empty gesture from a useless old fuck.

He stood there letting it bleed. Letting it hurt. Watching the blood spatter onto the white countertop and silvery shards of mirror for a long time before he finally grabbed a hand towel and wrapped the wounds.

CHAPTER 38

The man in black's head lolled on his neck, control of those muscles lost to him for the time being.

First it leaned his skull back about as far as it could, the top of his cranium touching the upholstery of the backseat where he reclined. Felt like he was getting laid out in a dentist's chair, someone sure to stick their hands in his mouth any minute now to root around for a bit.

Then, when he tried to correct this awkward positioning, he lost his balance again, lurching the other way like a listing ship, whole upper body slamming forward until he head-butted the back of the driver's seat. The impact stood him up a little, snapped his neck back like a rubber band, made his skull quiver.

It seemed, in that moment, about the funniest thing that had ever happened to him. Like he'd become a cartoon.

Strange laughs gurgled out from deep in his gullet, throaty chortles and snorts that sounded foreign to his ears. Almost sounded more porcine than human, a concept which made it impossible to stop the giggling.

The tears flowed now. Tears of joy, albeit a confused joy. A fucked-up kind of glee that came out of the nozzle of an aluminum can.

And then the laughing cut out. And everything went deathly quiet apart from the buzzing whoosh the poison he'd breathed seemed to beam into the air all around him.

He blinked a few times. Confused. Where the hell was he, again? He knew that he should know this, that it was important, but he squinted, gave it a hard think, and he had no fucking clue.

He gazed through the windshield. Eyes going wide as he took in the neat rows of palm trees staring back.

Then it hit. He'd parked in the lot of some apartment complex. Out of the way. A good spot to switch off his brain for a little bit. He was looking at some decorative landscaping. Tidy little clumps of saw palmetto and bougainvillea… his mind drifted then, hanging on the last word.

Bougainvillea.

Weird word. He mouthed each syllable slowly, stretching out the vowel sounds into something strange and nonsensical, which started the laughing all over again.

Something brushed against his lips, and he sat up a little. Remembered to pull the rag loaded with duster away from his mouth and nose. Threw the sopping thing onto the dash.

That was good. Sometimes he got confused. Forgot to do that. Breathed the crap in too long and passed out. One time he'd woken up face down in a puddle of his own vomit. No memory of arriving in that position. Not even terribly concerned about it until he cleaned it up some hours later and considered he may have come close to accidentally killing himself.

He tipped his head back, took a few breaths, happy to feel the fresh wind coming in, dry and non-chemical, even if he could only taste the tang of the duster clinging to his tongue and throat.

And some part of him tried to raise a flag of some kind. Tried to renew his earlier worry about something or other. Something he'd heard on the radio, he thought.

Again, he gave it a think, but his thinker wasn't operating so smoothly just now. It wasn't doing much at all. He knew that. He tried to figure a way to get this thing kick-started, jostle some thinking juice loose or something, but then he forgot what he was even trying for in the first place. Was there something he was trying to figure out? Trying to remember a song he'd heard on the radio or some shit like that, he thought, but that made no fucking sense.

He jolted upright again, eyes snapping to the foliage sprawled out beyond the windshield. Palm trees? Where the fuck was he?

He looked around the car again, reminding himself where he was. Apartment complex. Right, right.

The can of duster caught his eye on the floor, and he scooped it up without thinking. Aimed that nozzle into his mouth, lips wrapping around the thing, finger finding the trigger.

But no. No.

He dropped the can back to the floor. He was already good, he knew. The old thinker was shut down like he wanted, and it would be for a few hours now. If he sucked down anymore, he'd be out of his head for too long. Could be twelve hours or more before he was right again.

He couldn't have that.

He laid back, his body kind of falling into that dentist-chair-sprawl again, and he closed his eyes, and he listened to the whooshing and buzzing that he knew must not really be there.

He needed to stay sharp for tonight.

Yes. Tonight.

It was going to be a doozy, he thought.

And all the memories came to him. Pictures opening in his head. Gory, blood-smeared movies projected on the backs of his eyelids. All those wounds gouged into flesh by his blade. His mark left on the world again and again, one body at a time.

And the gore was to be continued, wasn't it? Yes, yes.

Tonight was going to be a bloodbath. A different kind of joy altogether.

CHAPTER 39

Loshak had just climbed into his rental — clean and bandaged and intent on driving around until he found something to eat — when his phone rang. It was Detective Renaud.

"We got a hit on the photo," he said without any preamble. "About two hours after it hit the internet and started circulating on TV, a gas station clerk called in. Apparently, our boy Eddie Zakarian goes into this specific Shell station every few nights to get a couple of microwave burritos. Usually late, around two or three a.m. It's the only thing open at that hour in that neighborhood."

Adrenaline surged through Loshak's veins, the steady *whump-whump* of his heartbeat picking up speed."Did you ask about a tattoo?"

"Night shift clerk confirmed our guy has one on the inside of his left forearm," Renaud said. "And I quote, 'A little cross thingy with an infinity symbol stuck to it.'"

Loshak's wrapped fist clenched involuntarily, all his wounds crying out in agony at the straining of the muscles, but he held it anyway. They had the bastard now. The clock was ticking down for Edward Zakarian."That's the good news," Renaud continued.

Loshak relaxed his fist, saw fresh spots of blood appear on the bandage where the cuts had reopened. "I take it that means there's bad news?"

"There was another murder over in Margate last night."

"Shit. Same M.O.?"

"Not exactly. That's what I wanted to ask you about, actually. It was outside of a bar, and it doesn't seem like robbery was the motive. Victim had almost two hundred bucks in his wallet," Renaud explained.

Loshak frowned down at his injured knuckles. The bloody bandage was really clashing with his tie. He'd have to go put on a fresh bandage now.

"What makes you think it was Zakarian?" he asked, sliding out of the car with the phone pressed to his ear.

"Couple of things," Renaud said. "First is that we got a second tip. Gal that tends bar at the place says she's pretty sure Zakarian was there last night."

"Pretty sure?"

"Only knows him by looks. It wasn't until she saw the stuff on TV about him that she connected him with the murder in the parking lot," Renaud explained. "The second thing is the attack itself. The victim had his throat slashed, and the medical examiner said the fatal wound was so deep, it was almost a complete decapitation."

The corners of Loshak's mouth curled down in disgust. "Well… that does sound like our guy."

"Yeah." There was a beat of silence over the line before Renaud spoke again. "So what do you think? That'd be a pretty big change in his – what do you call it – pattern, no? Would this guy really go from creeping into houses in the dead of night to slashing a guy's throat right out in the open? A place where people were bound to know his name or at least his face?"

Reaching his room, Loshak unlocked the door and pushed inside.

"It's definitely possible. Aggressive behavior like this has a way of escalating."

"So what is it? He thinks he's invincible now?" Renaud asked.

"Maybe in part. But I think these guys subconsciously know it can't go on forever. That it's only a matter of time before they get caught. Toward the end of Ted Bundy's career – if you can call it that – he assaulted five women in one night. It's a buildup of frustration, all that rage getting out of control like a wildfire. But in another way, I think they're flailing at the limits. Begging someone to stop them."

While Loshak talked, he unwound the blood-stained bandage, tossed it on the counter, and began re-wrapping his hand with a fresh length of gauze. It was an unwieldy task to complete while maintaining a phone conversation, but he managed.

Loshak finished the job and removed the phone from the awkward embrace between his chin and shoulder. "I assume you've got folks sitting on the gas station and the bar?"

"Yeah, though I'm not holding out much hope on the bar. He'd have to be a complete idiot to go back there," Renaud answered.

"You're probably right about that, though he might be curious enough to drive by. See the crime scene marked out with the yellow tape. These guys tend to revisit these places, revisit the violent moments, as often as they can."

A chill crept up Loshak's spine as he spoke these words. The reality that the killer was out there now seemed more real than ever. The agent pictured Zakarian moving through the city somewhere, aimlessly driving around under the swaying palm trees. Always moving. Always stalking. Those cold, black killer's eyes searching out his next score. His next victim.

"Make sure the guys keeping a lookout know what this guy is capable of. He is chaos personified. On top of that, there's a very real chance he'll be on something. Meth, speed, coke. An upper almost for certain. Zakarian should be approached with the utmost caution."

"Armed and dangerous," Renaud said. "They know."

But Loshak wasn't sure any of them really knew.

He'd seen firsthand the violence that particular brand of desperation could produce. Had witnessed the destruction left behind when law enforcement attempted to grab the tiger by the tail.

Even after the call ended, Loshak stood in the motel bathroom for some time, staring down at the wadded up bandage on the counter, at the bright red spots that had bled through.

They were so close. Never had they been closer.

So why did Loshak feel suddenly certain that things were about to go terribly wrong?

CHAPTER 40

The bright white lights of the gas station glared into the night, attracting crowds of bugs determined to throw themselves into the nonexistent fire inside. From the motel parking lot next door, with the windows on the rental car rolled down, Loshak could hear them plinking against the glass casings.

The lights attracted another kind of swarm, too. The all-nighters and the graveyard shift workers. People pumping gas, buying scratch-offs and cigarettes, single tallboys of malt liquor, or nachos and Styrofoam cups of Pepsi the size of five-gallon buckets.

When they'd first come on shift, Loshak and Spinks had perked up at every car that pulled in and every person who walked up. But the excitement wore off after the first hour, turning instead toward frustration and restlessness. Now a new face approaching the station was cause for contempt rather than exhilaration. And it wasn't even ten o'clock. Supposedly, Zakarian didn't usually show up until around three a.m.

Parked across the street was another undercover vehicle, with a third on the back side of the station. He wondered whether they were feeling the same restlessness. It seemed likely.

The best thing about this stakeout was that there hadn't been any time to think about the events at Jan's house. Instead, his thoughts churned with the particulars of the case, and the whole decapitated pup fiasco was pushed to a stale corner of his mind, along with the anger. Until Spinks got bored and started talking.

"Hey, my friend checked out your landlord buddy. Get this—"

"Forget it," Loshak said. "It's over."

"What's over?"

Loshak told Spinks about Roxie, about Jan finding her beloved little dog's head on her porch, about burying just that piece in a plastic garbage bag because they couldn't find the body, his voice flat and empty through the whole story. As he spoke, he could feel the anger simmering again. But it was just an old man's impotent rage. What was he going to do? Cut his hand on something else?

"Man," Spinks said, shaking his head. "That is fucked up."

Loshak shrugged. "Yeah, well. Jan's already packed. She's going to Norfolk to stay with her sister."

"So you're just gonna let him get away with this? No way, man."

"It's too late."

Spinks grinned, and in the light from the gas station, Loshak could see a glint of malice in the reporter's eyes.

"My motto is it's never too late to dish out some well-earned vengeance. If you let it go a little while, that just means they don't see it coming."

Spinks grabbed the console and dash, maneuvering himself around in the passenger seat so he was twisted toward Loshak.

"Listen to this: The house your ex-wife lives in? It was turned into a duplex without a permit. We report that, and this guy will owe thousands and thousands in penalties and back taxes. Sixteen years' worth! Way he explained it, the final sum would be close to six figures."

"Six figures? Jesus." Loshak smirked, then shook his head. "It's a lot. I know it is. But it doesn't feel like enough. Doesn't feel like an appropriate punishment for what he took away from her."

"Yeah, but it's some," Spinks argued. "You can't just let him get away with no punishment. Even if you can only wreak a little havoc, that's a little less shit that gets stood for in this world. One less person who just got away without having to pay any price for the evil he did."

Loshak nodded, scratching his jaw. But he pulled his fingers away when he felt the skin go all loose and the old man from the mirror flashed in his head again, the old man that was who he'd become.

"I want to do more," he said, aware how feeble that sounded. He struggled through a few even weaker thoughts, trying to explain. "Most of the time nowadays, I feel old. Useless. I didn't use to be this way. I know I didn't because I can remember what it felt like. It surprises me every time that I'm not still thirty. Or even forty. I do my job, keep my watch the best I can, but even that'll be over soon. Four years, to be exact."

Spinks cocked his head. "Got something big planned?"

"Mandatory age of retirement for the Bureau is fifty-seven," Loshak explained. "And when I'm done, it won't have mattered. However many murderers I help rip off the street, there will always be more. You take one down, ten pop up in his place. Crime's never going to stop. The cruelty and violence, it's always going to be out there. It never ends."

He fell silent as the image of that garbage bag rolled through his head. Not burying Jan's dog for her, burying its head. Just its head.

"Yeah, but what about that partner you mentioned," Spinks said. "Darger? She's going to be carrying the torch once you're gone, right?"

Loshak took a breath in and let it out. Didn't tell Spinks that Darger was off right now trying to decide if she even wanted to be a part of the FBI anymore. Didn't tell Spinks especially that lately he thought it would probably be better for Darger if she decided to quit now.

But Spinks wouldn't drop it. "What we're doing right here and now, going after this serial killer, that's good. We're doing good. We're going to stop him. Maybe another guy will start hacking people apart the day after we catch this Zakarian guy, maybe there are guys out there doing it right now and getting away with it. Maybe on a grand, cosmic scale, what we're doing doesn't make any difference. But to the dad whose kids don't get murdered in their beds tonight, whose wife doesn't get raped and strangled while he bleeds to death nearby, what we're doing makes all the difference."

Spinks sat back in his seat.

"There's no greater good you can do than that," the reporter said, nodding in agreement with himself. "You just keep fighting. Every day. All the time. I mean, what the hell else are you going to do?"

CHAPTER 41

After two full hours in the car, neither Loshak nor Spinks seemed able to sit completely still. They fidgeted, bounced their knees, sloshed loud gulps of bottled water down their gullets. Eventually, they'd turn to energy drinks of some kind to stay sharp. Coffee, at least. But for now, at just a quarter to midnight, it was water.

Talk radio murmured out of the speakers, local people sounding off about the serial killer now dominating the local news cycle. Some theories. Some rumors. Some tough talk. Regardless of the nature of the individual calls, naked fear underlaid all of them. Loshak could hear it as plain as anything.

It wasn't surprising to him. It was the standard human reaction to try to make sense out of this kind of chaos, to spit the theories out there where other people could agree with you or prove you wrong. The Miami area stations were probably getting bombarded with calls, one big peer review trying to break down this boogieman into human terms, make him less terrifying. And with the brutal murders front and center in everyone's minds, it only made sense that one or more of the station managers would try to cash in on the buzz. Broadcast the anxiety live on the air and milk it for all it was worth. Feed the fear machine. Why not?

Frantic voices spilled into the car's cabin. Fast talkers whose agitation seemed infectious.

"You neo-globalists just don't get it," a shaky voice said. "There's only one thing to be done with an animal like this sick cuck slithering into our homes at night. One thing."

Though clearly a man, the voice sounded unnatural. Thin and filtered into a tinny chirp that reminded Loshak of the old days. He snorted at the thought that maybe this kook was calling in from a landline. Probably from a bunker underground somewhere, his cranium firmly wrapped in either tinfoil or tinsel.

The caller ranted on.

"It ain't about compassion or a lack thereof. You can stuff your mercy in a sack for all it's good for. I'm talking about lethal injection, brother. A few thousand CCs of poison Kool-aid injected directly into this hombre's pecker. Send him to hell via instant intravenous delivery, you feel me? Skip the highway. Directly to Hell. Like, the body's still warm, and this guy is already getting anal-probed by the devil, OK? Might not be politically correct to say this kind of thing. Might offend some of the delicate sensibilities out there, but—"

Loshak flipped the radio off.

His eyes flicked to the gas station storefront where nothing moved. It'd probably be hours before Zakarian rolled this way — if he showed at all — and still all Loshak could do was watch the place, trying not to blink. A rack of potato chips stared back at him through the glass, Lays and Ruffles and tubes of Pringles. And past that, the hot case, nacho station, and microwave where a serial killer nuked his nightly burrito.

"Highway to Hell, huh?" Spinks said. "You think that's where our boy is headed?"

"Don't know. I guess that'd make sense for a final destination, but I'm not looking so far ahead just yet. I'm kind of hoping he swings by this establishment for a microwave burrito or two here pretty soon."

Spinks chuckled through his nostrils.

"I figure you've thought about that a lot, though, with your daughter and all. Where we go after, I mean. After this."

Loshak ruffled his fingers through his hair, leaving the top of it to stick out at odd angles. "Yeah, I guess I have."

"Same, same."

Spinks sat forward in his seat now, his eyes going a little wide. After all that talk radio, he seemed to be ready to rant a little himself.

"My wife believes in it all. Heaven, Hell, God, the Devil, all that stuff. To her, Davin's up there chilling with Jesus and my mom, waiting for us to get off our asses and die already. Not that believing that made it any easier losing him. But she's sure — absolutely, one-hundred-percent sure — that she's got it right."

Vinyl upholstery squeaked as he scooted around in the seat and adjusted his elbow on the console.

"Shit won't quite hold still for me, though," he said, now gesturing with little grabbing motions with his fingers. "It's one of those ideas that squirms and morphs every time I think about it — or so it seems, anyway. Sometimes, I guess I think it's nothing, you know. Life ends. Period. End of story."

With his hands, he mimicked the two halves of an open book slamming shut.

"The current in your brain winks out to black, and

there's nothing else. And I get why Lisa doesn't want to think that, because at first, that idea is terrifying. Who wants to think about their baby falling into darkness all by himself? Especially when you spend half their childhood calming their fears about the dark. But then I think about it more, and I realize that he never would've experienced it like that. By the time that fade to black happened, he was gone. And it'll be the same for me when I die. Same for you and everyone else. You're never awake in the dark. You're spared that, and when I think about it in those terms, then it seems OK in a way. Death is just the end. There's no suffering. It's a finality."

Spinks sat back again, this spouting of morbidity seeming to comfort him in some perverse way, Loshak thought. From the sound of it, he probably hadn't had much chance to talk it over with his wife. Maybe because they'd had fights about it before, maybe because he knew she wouldn't take the idea of her son just gone forever well. Whatever it was, Loshak was fine with letting him talk.

After the span of a few breaths, Spinks started talking again, but his voice was more subdued this time, a little distant.

"But other times I think maybe, somehow, it will be like before. I'll be back with my family, back with my son. Our lives, our familial existence, restored to how it was before things went wrong. I think that's probably what Lisa sees when she thinks of heaven, what she's hoping for. All three of us together. Living in the same little house. All the old wounds healed up. Our hearts made full again. No worries. Just a warm place to stay and be together. Forever, I guess."

Spinks blinked in the quiet a few times before he

finished his thought.

"It seems like that would be right, you know? Seems like that's how things ought to be. Wish I could believe it all the time is all."

They were quiet. The drone of the cars rushing past swelled to fill the silence between them. Loshak stared at the little mustached heads on all the cans of Pringles across the parking lot. He could tell from the corner of his eye that Spinks was watching the store as well.

"What about you?" Spinks said after a time, still staring out at nothing.

"What about me?"

"You believe in any kind of heaven or what have you?"

Loshak hesitated a beat before he answered.

"In a way, yeah. Yeah, I do. But I think maybe what exists beyond this world is just energy, you know? Nothing more. Nothing less. Because physics tells us that energy is infinite. It cannot be created or destroyed. So I guess I think we all go back to where we came from. The force that animates us, I guess you could say. We go back to the well of where that life comes from, and we're no longer separate from each other the way we are here on this plane. No longer animals. Reduced to that essence of life, reduced to energy. And all the drama we experience here is over, the conflict, all the territorial battling we do is rendered meaningless. We are no longer burdened with these concerns of power or control. We simply exist. Maybe that's heaven. Or maybe it's something else. I'm not sure."

Spinks blinked a few times, eyebrows slowly crushing together.

"So like... where would you live? In this energy that

we're all in together, I mean. What are the living arrangements in that type of operation?"

"Well, no. It's not like that," Loshak said. "We wouldn't be corporeal, I guess. Energy, right? Just energy."

Spinks was quiet for a second. His eyebrows remained furrowed.

"So we're like a big ball of light or something?"

"No." Loshak shifted in his seat. "I mean, I don't know. This is just what makes sense to me."

"A big ol' ball of light, huh? I mean, I guess it could make sense, but… wave or particle?"

Loshak snorted. "Look, I'm not trying to convert you to my religion or anything here. Just making idle chitchat."

"No, it's fine," Spinks said, shaking his head. "I asked. You answered."

A car pulled into the gas station lot, and a lady with a big perm got out and hustled inside. She seemed in a real hurry. Probably some cigarette or lotto ticket emergency, Loshak thought.

Still, he watched Spinks out of the corner of his eye, had a feeling the reporter had more to say on the subject of the afterlife, and after a few seconds, he did.

"You always go abstract with this stuff, you know that?" Spinks said. "Whether we're talking about the afterlife or people or anything. Always abstract."

He wheeled his head to look at Loshak for the first time in a while, and his gaze stayed trained on the agent as he went on.

"I think that says something about you, man. I'm not judging, mind you. You're good at what you do and everything. But always with the abstract. Reducing reality to concepts and feelings and balls of twinkly light. There's a real world right here in front of you, you know. Territory. People. A physical universe you can live in, act in, exert your will upon. Something beyond ideas and theories and conjecture."

Loshak shrugged. "The ideas, the theories and conjecture, that's a necessary step, though. It has to happen so we can find these murderers. You can't get to the concrete without going through the abstract first."

"Yeah, but seems to me like you get stuck on that step," Spinks said. "Trapped up in your head to the point that you feel powerless, helpless. And you forget, maybe, that, you know, you're a quite corporeal dude at the moment — a man of the law, even — and you're living in a material world where life and death, justice and injustice lay within an arm's length if you reach out for 'em. If you actually use your hands."

CHAPTER 42

When the duster wore off, the hunger finally got the better of the man in black. Time had ceased to mean anything. It was all one long, empty second full of need. Craving. And it was only getting worse. He scratched at his crawling scalp, dirt and sweat building up beneath his fingernails, and oil slicking his palms.

Huffing the duster had passed the time, just the way he knew it would — a joyous confusion occupying him for a few hours, disconnecting his head from the rest of his body. But it had also hollowed him out. Left him feeling empty, cold, lonesome as hell.

He pulled up to a stoplight, made eye contact with himself in the rearview mirror. Who was this creature staring back at him with black pits for eyes? Maybe he would never know. Maybe no one would.

Movement at the bottom of the mirror caught his attention, pulled his gaze downward. A trickle of darkness fluttering out of his nostrils.

He touched his fingers to it, felt the sticky warmth. He already knew, but brought his hand into the wedge of light offered by an overhead streetlamp anyway. His fingertips glittered wet and red. A nosebleed.

He dug in the glove compartment, found a brown paper napkin, and applied it to the leaking holes in his face. The paper was harsh against his skin, a little gritty. And he watched it soak up his bodily fluid, dark splotches absorbing into the napkin and spreading like spilled ink.

Nosebleeds always made him feel like his body was falling apart. A fragile thing coming undone from the inside. Splitting open and crumbling to pieces like cracks in the sidewalk. Life seeping out from the broken places.

But when he pulled the napkin away, all signs of the blood were gone, and soon the worry dissipated, too.

And now the car was moving forward again, pressing into the darkness outside, headlights gouging the black with their glow.

And his hand tremored lightly against the wheel. Small twitches assailing his flesh, little jolts of energy that moved his muscles against his will.

And his chest trembled with surges of wet electricity every time he inhaled. Anticipation. Restlessness. Frustration threatening with every breath.

He needed drugs. Needed them.

Needed to get doped as soon as possible. Needed the next gram. Needed to get ripped. Needed to get fucked up.

The duster had passed the time, but now cocaine was calling him again. Begging him. His mistress. His true love. Making his body ache. Making sweat sheen everywhere.

He would get another haul tonight, dispatching whoever got in his way, and with the help of the white powder, he would pull Heaven back down and hold it in his head for a while again, hold it there for as long as he could.

He didn't realize it at the top of his mind, but he'd been circling back toward the Shell station as he got more and more agitated, his body crying out not only for the rush of cocaine in his veins but the weight of something hot in his stomach. In the absence of one, he was absolutely going to have the other. He couldn't purchase his next round of bliss for a few hours yet at the soonest, but sustenance? A warm meal? That he could have. And so he would.

He caught sight of the burning white lights ahead like an urban lighthouse and stepped on the gas.

CHAPTER 43

Shift change rolled around at one. Plenty of time to get the new undercover vehicles settled in before their killer showed up at his accustomed three.

Except tonight, the replacements were late. The guys in the other two cars had been chattering about it back and forth for the last five minutes.

Loshak reminded himself that these guys had wives and families to get back to, or at the very least a cat to feed. They'd just sat through five boring hours of disappointment and frustration; waiting for their replacements who should've been there fifteen minutes back was just the icing on the turd.

He reached under his dash and pulled up the handset.

"This is Car Two," he said, breaking into their conversation. "Why don't you guys go ahead and take off. Our guy probably won't be here for another couple hours. Spinks and I can hold down the fort for these next few minutes. We'll keep an eye out until the fresh eyes show up."

Car Three didn't have to be told twice. They thanked Loshak and drove off.

But Car One hesitated.

"You sure?" the officer asked. Loshak searched his mental Rolodex for a name and came up with Proper.

"My wife thinks I'm with a hooker, so I'm good for another hour at least," Spinks said.

Loshak hit the Talk button again, smirking. "Go on home and get some rest. We'll sleep in tomorrow to make up the difference."

"All right," car one said. "Heading out."

The Tahoe across the street flicked on its headlights, then pulled out of its parking space and into the sparse traffic.

"A hooker?" Loshak said, shaking his head.

Spinks grinned. "Don't be jealous just because you're not funny and I am. I was a skinny, four-eyed black nerd in the projects. It was be funny or get your head kicked in. Not like any of the gangs would have me. Had to improvise, you know? What you're hearing right now is all survival skill."

Loshak laughed through his nose, his chest juddering as the puffs of air whispered out.

"Of course, I had some inborn talent, but…" Spinks went on. "See, before my dad ran off and Mom and me moved into Liberty City, I lived in Palmetto Bay. I was going to a prep school where the eggiest of eggheads didn't care for my nosy little punk-ass, either. Especially not ones who told the teachers when they caught you smoking under the bleachers. But you figure out how to slide past their defenses. Get 'em laughing, and you can move in with any crowd you want to. Funny is like camouflage. Doesn't matter if you're dealing with rich folk or poor folk, funny works on just about all of 'em."

A dark sedan pulled into the Shell, parking at the curb. Loshak was only half-looking at it, convinced it was just another random citizen on their way to the late shift.

"And it affords you the ability to be brutally honest with

people when no one else can," Spinks was saying. "It's like how the court jester was the only guy who could tell the king to his face that he was a fat asshole with bad breath without being executed. He could do that because he could get the king to laugh at it like it was all some big joke."

The door on the dark sedan opened, and for some reason, Loshak found himself holding his breath. A younger man in a black t-shirt and black pants climbed out, scratching at a head of stringy, greasy hair.

Loshak gripped the armrest and sat forward in his seat. "It's him. That's Zakarian."

CHAPTER 44

Loshak eased the door open and climbed out of the car. Slow. Casual. Hand slipping inside his jacket to unsnap his holster. His eyes bored into the back of Zakarian's head, trained on the killer like laser sights.

He heard Spinks' door open. From the corner of his eye, he saw the reporter rising, getting out. Loshak wanted to hiss at Spinks to sit down, stay put, but a more urgent instinct kept his mouth shut. Something primitive, from the predatory side of his brain, the part of him that felt like a lion creeping through the grass toward an unsuspecting gazelle.

His pulse hammered in his neck. Adrenaline pumped out to his arms and legs, hot and blue-white. Everything sharpened — the scrape of his shoes on the asphalt, the rolling scuff of tires as an orange crossover pulled out of the gas station. Music from the street, following the Doppler curve as a little red car passed. Whitesnake again. Was Florida experiencing some sort of hairband revival or was it just his Uber driver out cruising the streets in the middle of the night?

Under the bright stadium lights of the gas station, Zakarian stood hunched next to his open car door, chin tucked to his chest. He fiddled with something in his pocket, then slammed his car door, and headed for the building.

Loshak crossed the motel parking lot, trying to keep his

strides smooth, his speed even. Moderate, but not hasty. If Zakarian had caught a glimpse of the news today or turned on his car radio at any point over the last eleven hours — maybe to blast some Whitesnake — he would know they were circulating his name and face. He'd be on high alert, ready to run. Or fight.

Though the scrawny kid with the greasy hair approaching the gas station for his nightly burrito didn't look as if he were on high alert. Loshak suspected the confidence was a combination of the drugs and the familiarity of the place. Maybe he'd even been drawn here because it was safe, part of his routine, and therefore sacrosanct from threats.

Zakarian stepped up onto the sidewalk, chopping his steps as he came to the glass double doors and twisting his shoulders a little to reach for the Shell-shaped handle.

Loshak cleared the concrete bumper cut through the grass between the motel parking lot and the gas station. The sundried blades crunched under his weight.

Suddenly, Zakarian straightened, hand falling away from the door handle. He spun to his right and veered off toward the east of the building, disappearing around the side.

Dropping all pretense, Loshak darted after him. Spinks' footsteps slammed into the ground right behind him. Had Zakarian seen them? Heard them? Somehow felt their presence? Had the hairs on the back of his neck stood up, sensing Loshak's stare like a zebra suddenly aware it was being stalked by a lion?

The soles of his loafers skidded a little on the wet asphalt as he made the turn around the corner of the building. On the wall, a gray steel door slammed shut with a combination *thud-clang*. A sign for Restrooms hung overhead.

Loshak pulled his Glock and grabbed the smooth metal door handle. A glance back at Spinks. Then he jerked the door open.

It led into a little square room with two more doors — the left one Men's and the right Women's. Loshak hesitated. Heard Spinks' harsh breath practically in his ear.

Men's, he decided.

Loshak crashed through the door, letting it rebound off the wall and hit him in the back as he cleared the bathroom, swinging his gun from left to right. Two calcium-stained sinks under broken, dirty mirrors. A matching set of urinals on the opposite wall, separated by a single grimy window. In the far corner, a line of gray stalls covered in scratched and markered graffiti. Overhead, fluorescent bulbs flickered and hummed.

No people.

Spinks ducked down to check the floor. He came back up with a shrug and gestured to the stall doors.

Loshak nodded, catching the drift of the reporter's thoughts: No feet, but that didn't mean he wasn't standing on the toilets.

Loshak moved to the first door at a creep. Paused. Leaned back, brought his leg up, and kicked it open.

It slammed off the toilet paper holder. Empty except for a clogged toilet.

Next stall. Loshak didn't hesitate this time, just kicked the door in.

It was empty, too.

He was squaring up to the third stall when they heard it. The crash of shattering glass muffled by the cinderblock wall.

The sound of Zakarian breaking out the window in the Women's restroom.

CHAPTER 45

Loshak left the bathroom at a sprint, steel doors crashing open as he slammed out into the arc lights holding back the darkness. He took off around the back of the station, heading for the bathroom windows. Spinks' footsteps echoed behind him as he ran.

Then the reporter was pulling ahead, younger, faster. Loshak opened his mouth to shout out a warning — he hadn't seen any weapons on Zakarian, but the danger was still there — but Spinks rounded the corner before Loshak could choke out a word.

Zakarian was waiting just out of sight, ready to pounce. He leapt on Spinks like a cougar, a vicious tackle that snapped the reporter's head around on his neck. They hit the ground and skidded, the killer on top.

Startled, Loshak missed the step down from the sidewalk and tripped. His ankle rolled inward, and he crashed down to hands and knees, biting his tongue. Tasting blood.

For a second he thought he'd dropped his gun, and he felt the humiliation pour in, filling up his skull and all down his spine like cerebral fluid, pounding in his temples. But no, the Glock was still there in his hand.

He shook the embarrassment and anger off, lifting his head just in time to see the killer perched on Spinks' chest.

Zakarian lifted his arm over his head, and time slowed to a crawl. Loshak saw the blade clenched in his fist, a

232

jagged folding knife made for skinning game or cutting rope. An outdoorsman's knife. The blade, dark with dried blood, arced down toward Spinks.

Loshak felt like he was stuck in a dream, caught in a pit of quicksand and unable to move in anything but slow motion. He pushed himself up to his knees, raising his gun.

But Zakarian ripped forward, throwing his skeletal body weight behind the knife as he plunged it into Spinks.

Loshak heard Spinks hiss out a raspy noise. Pained. Choked and wet. He swore he could smell the blood let from the reporter's neck, a coppery scent gushing and wafting there from a wound somewhere beneath the killer's frame.

The agent raised the Glock. Lined his sights up with Zakarian's back. Swallowed what felt like a tennis ball lodged in his throat.

Time slowed further, the world reduced to crawling frame by frame. Loshak could feel every little constriction of his heart in his chest. Could hear the blood swishing in his ears, the beat of his pulse laid down under that wet sound like drums.

The gun fluttered there before him. Arms shaking like crazy. Old man arms. Weak and palsied.

A breath sucked into his lungs and held there. He tried to steady himself. Tried to calm the twitching muscles in his back and arms for just these next few seconds.

It was now or never.

He squeezed the trigger and the muzzle blazed and popped. The Glock jerked in his hands like a wild thrashing thing trying to escape his grip. He held on.

But the shot went wide. Not even close.

And panic gripped Loshak by the shoulders, by the waist, by the scruff of the neck.

He felt like he was looking at the world cross-eyed. Everything a little blurred, a little wonky and out of focus.

The silence after the crack of the gunfire seemed impossible. Empty nothingness hung up in the air all around them.

Loshak couldn't think. Couldn't breathe. Couldn't stop that shaking in his arms. He was in a nightmare. This couldn't be real.

Zakarian whirled off of Spinks. Lurched into some aggressive stance with his feet set wider than his shoulders. Hesitated for the briefest moment. And charged. Barreling straight toward Loshak, head and shoulders lowered like he meant to bash heads with the kneeling agent.

The recoil had rocked the gun up, lifted Loshak's arms out of position, but he couldn't think straight now. Could barely see straight. He made no correction as he squeezed off several more shots, trying to stop the oncoming psychopath.

Every single shot went high and wide.

And Zakarian just kept coming. Knife splayed at his side. Death in those black, cold eyes.

Then the Glock jammed. Failure to feed.

Some part of Loshak's brain knew this was an easy fix. Knew it'd happened multiple times on the range. That all he needed to do was rack the slide and try again.

Tap. Rack. Bang.

But these thoughts couldn't be heard over the screaming panic making his brain quiver, the temporary autism denying him access to much of his mind.

Loshak was blind. No longer thinking. Reduced to a terrified child.

Powerless.

Helpless.

His finger kept squeezing the trigger even though it wasn't resetting, gun clicking uselessly in his hands, his heart trying to leap out of his chest. He couldn't stop. That dark figure was slithering closer and closer, ready to sink the blade into his throat.

Zakarian stopped suddenly, just out of arm's reach. The knife was still raised in a threat. His head tilted slightly, like a curious dog, causing stringy hair to hang down over his right shoulder.

Loshak didn't even think. He stopped trying to shoot, sitting there on his knees, and lifted his hands into the air.

Surrendering. Submitting. Giving up.

Their eyes met, one set black and cold, the other pale and scared.

Then Edward Zakarian turned and ran into the night.

CHAPTER 46

Zakarian burst through a barrier of pines and low palm trees at the back of the gas station lot, the sharp leaves and scratchy needles tearing at his face and bare arms. He didn't slow, sprinting recklessly into the darkest shadows, accelerating as the branches whipped around him like outstretched arms.

For a time his camera saw only the vaguest sense of movement in the dark, a shifting blackness all around him like a chasm, a vortex, a portal opening to swallow him up. And he was scared again, and small. Adrift in the nothingness. So far gone in the darkness that he couldn't imagine a way out. Not anymore.

Lost.

But he tucked his chin against his chest and the ground brought him back to reality. The slight wetness reflected from the grass sliding by underfoot. Just seeing the shimmer of it rooted him once more in the physical world.

The hedge let out into some kind of alley, then dumped him in a residential area full of heavily fortified crack houses and crumbling sidewalks.

Good. This would work.

His heart still galloped in his chest, but the fear had given way to a sick kind of excitement. The thrill of a chase, of a hunt. Adrenaline. The rush reminded him of coke, of the euphoria of breaking into someone's house, crossing that threshold into a private residence, never knowing who might live or die in the next fifteen minutes. Jacked out of his mind on that sick anticipation.

Time to let those animal instincts take over, same as any other night on the prowl. Time to prove himself the most aggressive, the most brutal beast in this jungle again… or die trying.

He cut through a slender patch of dead grass between two houses, listening to the thump of bass and the muffled sound of yelling through the wall to his right.

Cars and trucks were parked up in the yard and on the street around the party house. Enough to make him feel like they were creating a buffer between him and the cops at the gas station. Another stroke of luck, that. Good.

He forced himself to slow down to a walk. His blood was pumping through his veins at triple-speed, his skin glistening with rank sweat. His muscles twitched and jittered, little screwbolts of adrenaline still twisting into them, sending electrical shocks spiraling along every nerve in his body. He twisted his head from side to side, cracking his neck, and tried to relax his shoulders.

Everybody in the whole world was looking for him now, hunting him instead of the other way around. He had to act normal. Natural. Nonchalant. No more running in a blind panic. He had to keep his head down and find a place to hide out. Find a car. Or a gun. Or both.

Shit. One thing at a time. Hide first.

A house across the street caught his eye. Two-story, bigger than the rest of these dumps. Windows open to let in the cool night breeze.

The two upper-level windows were evenly spaced over the garage, and something about the layout gave the impression that the house was smiling at him.

He veered toward it, smiling back.

CHAPTER 47

Loshak slumped on the asphalt, the wetness from the afternoon rains soaking into the legs of his slacks, the humidity pressing into his face, plastering his button down and suit jacket to his chest and back and pits. Even in the middle of the night, the Florida heat didn't let up. It clutched at him, swaddled him, suffocated him. There was no relief in this place, ever. Not here, and not in life.

Sweat slicked his entire body, not just from the heat, but from the panic, the fear. Its sheen made him feel swampy and disgusting and small.

He looked up at the bugs swarming the arc lights overhead. Idiot things bashing themselves face-first into the bulb over and over.

He'd pussed out. A coward. When the moment came to assert himself, he put his hands up. Left himself at the mercy of a serial killer. Survived through sheer dumb luck.

It was like the truth Spinks had talked about in their first meeting. Going off the facts, anybody would see Loshak as some star FBI profiler, an author of a couple bestselling true crime books, and a badass who took down the worst of the worst criminals out there. Those facts could look good, perhaps, on paper. But the truth was something different entirely, wasn't it?

He was an old man who panicked, who tripped and fell and missed every single shot, who choked when his friend was being attacked, who all but pissed his pants when the

239

killer locked eyes with him.

This world, this life had passed him by at some point. He was a shell of what he'd been all those years ago, back when those facts were accurate, back when he was a hard-nosed agent really making a difference in the world.

Somewhere along the way, he'd gone soft. Gotten old. Become an empty husk of himself.

His expiration date was up.

That was the truth.

So why did he keep going?

He was old and used up. Spent. Ready to be put down.

He blinked. Saw only the hollow sky above. And the bugs churned and buzzed as always, indifferent to anything but the lights they worshiped.

Pain fluttered in Loshak's chest. Sharp, stabbing. A tendril of hurt snaked down his left arm. He grabbed at it.

Jesus Christ. A heart attack. The final nail of humiliation, that last little stab of merciless truth. Going out exactly the way old men did.

But after a few seconds, the pain passed. Eased and disappeared. It was only panic. Anxiety. A truth, but not a fact.

Loshak stirred. Sat up. And the scuffle of his shoes on asphalt pulled him out of his tunnel vision.

Spinks.

Loshak's eyes locked on the crumpled form only a few yards away. The reporter was lying still now, his body splayed on the asphalt as blood seeped out around his head.

CHAPTER 48

In the kitchen of the big house, Zakarian shifted back into the man in black, the demon that stalked the nights, bringing death and destruction wherever he roamed. He squatted down, out of the glare of streetlights coming through the open window behind him, and let his eyes adjust to the darkness.

Little by little, his breathing slowed, and the panic of the confrontation bled out of him. Replaced by seething, animal rage. An aggression so sharp that it ached for expression. Violence.

The man in black wanted to kill. Needed to communicate that ultimate dominion over life and death, to remember what it felt like to hold that power in his hands.

He let the fury fully take hold of him, a hateful warmth creeping into his core and spreading down his limbs, tinting everything red. It felt good, felt right.

He knew what to do now. No longer needed to think.

And in flashes all the old feelings were there, too. The desperate feelings – the pain, the fear, the torments that had scarred him, damaged him beyond hope – they were all right there with him. Cold, cold feelings. But they couldn't compete with the heat surging through his veins now. Nothing could.

At last, he began to move. His feet slipped over the tiles and into a hallway, soundless in the inky shadow. Pictures flashed in his head, the things he needed: car keys, a gun, some basement or shed to hunker down in if he couldn't get a car fast enough.

He took a step down into a room lined on three walls with bookshelves. Near the middle, he could make out the vague shape of a sectional. Over by the window, a huge desk. He smelled cigars and leather, but couldn't tell whether it was a phantom memory of a scent or if the smell was just so powerful even his coke-rotted sinuses could pick it up.

Weird shapes stuck out of the shelf-less wall. Protruding and poking into the air, pointed racks of antlers jutting out. Animal heads. Stuffed and mounted and staring with sightless eyes.

It was a den, a man cave. The resident must be some kind of hunter.

The man in black smiled. He knew what that meant.

The gun safe was nestled among the bookshelves, a tall metal cabinet with a number padlock. There would be rifles in there and ammo for every occasion.

But Zakarian slithered over to the desk first. If he didn't find car keys thrown onto the flat surface along with the daily mail or stashed in one of the drawers, maybe he would find a scrap of paper with the code for the gun safe.

Printouts were scattered across the desktop, most of them driving directions. Beneath them was a closed laptop, its charging light blinking away. The butt of a fat stogie sat in a metal ashtray shaped like a cowboy hat, soggy and chewed. No keys.

Zakarian opened the top drawer, ready to rifle through pens and Post-its and paper clips. And there it was sitting in its own little custom foam-lined section, between a rainbow assortment of highlighters and three spare magazines.

A handgun.

CHAPTER 49

Snoring. Faint but there.

Something small slept in the next room over. It was too much, too convenient.

The man in black smiled so big his cheeks ached, little muscle tremors making the wet corners of his mouth twitch, tongue flicking out to feel his own flesh shudder from a different angle.

Stimulated. Entertained.

The killer crept out of the den and glided across the hall. The door to the room was already cracked, a nightlight in the form of a little brown truck with bucked teeth lighting up the racecar-shaped bed. A small head with black curls lay on the pillow, all the covers kicked off. Soft little belly poking out between a matching pajama top and bottoms, rising and falling with the snores.

The little boy was another obvious sacrifice meant for him, left to the slaughter. Tiny, helpless. Inevitable. Meant to be.

The gun would be too loud. Too easy. He slid the knife from his jeans, pulling it out slowly to let the anticipation last, excitement tingling along his nerves.

This kill would make things right. All things. It would prove his strength again. Prove his power. Prove he was protected so long as he showed no weakness.

He stepped into the room, knife trembling with excitement at the end of his outstretched arm, ready to rip away another life.

CHAPTER 50

Loshak scrambled over to Spinks' body on his hands and knees.

"Spinks?"

The reporter lay motionless, eyes staring out at nothing. A pool of blood surrounded his upper body, but the chest rose and fell. Loshak searched out the pulse on Spinks' neck. Thready and fast. Shock.

"Spinks, are you okay?"

No response, not even a blink.

Loshak studied his friend's head and chest. Looked like the wound was in the trapezius, the swell of muscle on either side of the neck. Missed his throat by an inch. Lucky. There was a serious gash there, Spinks definitely needed stitches, but it didn't look life-threatening.

"Talk to me, man," Loshak said, raising his voice.

He touched the shoulder opposite the stab wound. Spinks' shirt was soaked through with sweat, and clammy. Almost cold. It was the adrenaline and the shock, slowing down his bleed.

Just then, Spinks groaned, and his eyelids fluttered, a touch of lucidity returning to them.

Loshak's shoulders slumped with relief. He wiped his hand down the side of his face, slicking away sweat.

"What happened?" Spinks asked, looking around as if he wasn't sure where he was.

"It's okay," Loshak said. "You're going to be okay.

You've been stabbed — he stabbed you and then he ran off. But you're going to be okay."

More blinking. Spinks shook his head, then grabbed onto Loshak's shoulder and hauled himself up to sitting.

"Where is he? Did you get him?"

Loshak grimaced. "Like I said, he took off."

"So go get him," Spinks said.

"Are you sure you're okay?"

"I mean, you just told me fifteen times that I was."

Loshak took a breath and blew it back out. He was no action hero. His partner, Darger, she did that sort of thing, running after the killers and fighting them to the death. That physicality, it wasn't him, even in his youth. Now that he was old and tired? Forget it.

He knew the guy's psychology, though. That was his one and only advantage.

His gut told him Zakarian was still close. Probably within a few blocks. The chaotic types, they tended to rage out when they felt out of control. Tried to exert power over their situation through violence. The logical thing to do would be to steal a car and vacate the area as fast as possible. But guys like Zakarian responded emotionally, got all charged up, all hot and bothered, and logic went out the window. Anger. Hatred. Expressions of their strength. They slipped into rampage mode and more often than not got themselves caught.

It was a long shot, perhaps, but it felt right. And right now, his hunch was their best chance.

He hooked a finger at Spinks.

"Put some pressure on that wound, and call 9-1-1. Can you do that?"

Spinks blinked. Nodded.

"You sure you can remember how to dial and everything?"

A ghost of a smile pulled at the sides of Spinks' mouth. "Yeah. I think I can handle it."

Knees creaking, Loshak pushed himself up to standing and jogged toward the pines at the back of the gas station lot. He couldn't sprint. He wasn't some young rookie, running on grit and determination. He needed to go slow and steady to win this race.

He might not be able to run this guy down and overpower him, but outsmart him? Well, that was something he might be able to do.

CHAPTER 51

Zakarian limped out the front door into the night, holding
a hand towel to his bleeding thigh with one hand and
trying to shrug on a jacket he'd found with the other. It
wouldn't conceal the blood on his pants or the smears on
his hands, but those were harder to discern in the orangey
glow of the streetlight.

The blood was flowing pretty good from that opened
up place in his thigh, but he felt strong. He felt good. He
had everything under control now, the whole world back
under his thumb where it belonged.

Flashes of the kill came to him, but everything was a
little confused. The scenes rushed and out of order.

The knife plunging into that soft gut, thrusting and
ripping.

Blood rushing out faster than what seemed possible.
Hot and red.

The little eyes and mouth opened so wide. So scared.

And the boy cried out, a weak, tiny sound like a kitten
getting its tail pinched.

Zakarian had cried like that. How many times had he
whimpered in the night, begging for somebody to save
him? And nobody came. Nobody. Just like nobody came to
save this little lamb.

And then a jump cut to the little arms and legs
thrashing. A bloody foot connecting with Zakarian's knife
hand, the heel pounding like a hammer, driving the sharp

edge into his thigh.

Zakarian's eyes went wide as the pain hit. Sharp. A feeling like his leg was peeling apart. The wound looked like a gaping mouth in the dark.

The little fucker had been a fighter. Hadn't done him much good, though.

The man in black had found a pair of keys on the way out, hanging by the door. The fob said Toyota, but there wasn't a car in the driveway. He limped to the row of vehicles lining the street, all of them tinted yellow by the pole lights overhead. He couldn't tell the Fords from the Hyundais from the Chevies. They could all be Toyotas for all he knew. No way to tell which one might go with the key in his hand.

And as he stepped onto the asphalt, another round of memories assailed him. Murder pictures filling his head.

His long fingers encircled the little throat. Squeezed.

The chest bucked against his forearms, desperate for air. But the man in black decided who breathed and who suffocated. He was the ruler over life and death. He was the power in the darkness. No longer weak and scared and small, but huge, filling up every corner of the room with his strength.

Thin nails raked across Zakarian's face. Lines of humiliation more than pain. Red bloomed in his brain, hatred, fury. He was the aggressor, he was the attacker. The predator didn't get hurt, not by the prey.

Furious, he slammed the curl-laden head against a dresser. It crunched.

Movement across the street brought him back to the present. Just a flicker of shadows at first, and then a porch light flicked on.

A small group spilling out of the party house, to smoke on the porch. Three men around his age from the looks of them, somewhere in their twenties, two of them holding beer bottles.

Zakarian's heart hammered in his chest. Were they watching him? Did they see him come out of the big house? He had to get out of there.

He pressed a button on the key fob.

A RAV4 across the street beeped, flashing its lights. Right in front of the smokers' porch.

All three smokers craned their necks, searching out the source of the noise.

Zakarian froze. Looked at the ground. His free hand fumbled at his waistband, going for the gun, but it stopped shy of pulling it out. The cops from the gas station would be close by now, closing in on him. Probably just a block or two off. Firing a shot now would be a mistake unless he absolutely had to.

He swallowed, moved toward the car as if he didn't notice them. He reached for the driver's side door. Locked. He hit another button on the fob, and the locks opened with a *clunk*.

But one of the smokers stepped off the porch and onto the lawn.

"Hey, who the fuck are you?" the guy yelled. "That ain't your ride. It don't belong to you. Fuck off before we call the cops."

Neighbors, Zakarian thought. They must know the people in the house he just left.

Now all of them had descended from the porch. They

were creeping across the lawn, trying to corner him against the car. His fingers tightened around the gun's grip.

"Jesus, is that blood? He's fucking covered in it."

One of the men pointed. "Oh shit, it's that guy! The guy from the news. Zakarian the barbarian. Fuckin' serial killer."

Panic flooded in. He faltered, terrified. As if on cue, sirens wailed.

Fuck. They were close. Too close.

He backed up a step, then turned. Ran.

"Hey, where—" One of the smokers shouted. "Get back here!"

But he was gone, halfway down the block, the fear adding speed to his escape. He threw the RAV4's keys down. He had to find another car. Get out of here.

The words thundered in his head like galloping hooves as he ran: *Get out of here. Get out of here. Get out of here.*

CHAPTER 52

Bright jolts of pain shot through Loshak's bruised knees as he jogged, and the right one clicked with every step. His breath rushed in and out, harsh, loud. His mouth dried out from panting in this heat.

What the hell was he doing, chasing after this guy? Trying to be some big shot? He was fifty fucking three years old, for crying out loud. What was he going to do when he caught up to Zakarian, shake his cane at him?

The image of Jan crying flashed through his mind, her features helpless with rage. Then Shelly closing her eyes for that last time, nothing left of his daughter but her already skeletal shell. The look on Darger's face when he'd explained to her that, more often than not, corruption won. That little yappy dog's head pulling the garbage bag taut with its weight.

He hadn't been able to do anything about any of it. Failure after failure. It was all hurt and frustration and emptiness. More and more the older he got. If he survived tonight, there would just be something new and awful to face tomorrow. It never ended.

Somewhere up ahead, he heard voices shouting.

Behind him, sirens cut through the night.

Loshak picked up the pace. Pushed himself harder. It was all he could do.

CHAPTER 53

Zakarian's head tingled, his vision fluttering along the edges. Running seemed to open up the wound in his leg, and he'd lost the towel. Blood was flowing down the inside of his thigh like piss, hot against his clammy skin.

Adrenaline was the only thing keeping him upright at this point. The chemicals keeping him alert, pushing him through the wooziness.

He needed to slow down, stop and try to staunch the flow of blood, but he could hear the smokers behind him somewhere, their footsteps slapping against the street. Yelling every now and then. They had probably called him in, too, the fuckers.

At least he was pulling away. If he got crafty, he could hide maybe, and lose them.

The sidewalk in front of him swam away for a second, then came back.

Shit. He shook his head hard, trying to clear it. Sweat ran into his eyes, but he felt cold. His whole body was shivering.

He had to go, had to move. He put on a burst of speed, sprinting to widen the gap, then swerved down a driveway.

Out of nowhere, he slammed into something and bounced off, a metallic tinkling sound filling his ears. He blinked. He didn't remember closing his eyes, but he must have.

Chain link fence hovered inches from his face, and

beyond it, a little metal shed. The kind people stashed their lawn mowers in.

Zakarian grabbed the links and pulled himself up and over, falling into the grass and dog shit on the opposite side. He rolled to his knees and scrambled across the lawn. The shed door creaked when he jerked it open, but he managed to slide inside and get it shut again before the smokers saw him.

He felt around as his eyes adjusted to the darkness. It was a workshop, not a mower shed. A bench covered in tools and dirt along one wall. Metal shelves covered in junk along the other. He limped to the back wall where a single square window looked out into the night. Nothing but chain link and a view of the neighbor's backyard.

He leaned against the wall facing the door and pulled his stolen gun out. Waiting. Ready. But as he calmed, he could hear them out there, yelling at each other, searching for him. It didn't sound like they were getting closer to the shed. It sounded like they were passing by.

CHAPTER 54

A crowd of people milled about on either side of the street ahead, a group of them actually in the street. Loshak jogged toward them, knowing it had to be about Zakarian. The killer had been through here, left destruction and panic in his wake.

Two people were coming out of a house, a woman and a man. The man carried something in his arms. A bundle with bits hanging down limply like a dead octopus with only four legs.

Then Loshak was close enough to see the tiny hand, and he couldn't unsee it, couldn't look away. It was a kid. Clearly dead. Covered in blood.

Something Spinks had said rattled through Loshak's head. Tragedy comes along without warning and rips your life up. Does permanent damage. You can never heal quite right, you know?

The parents were arguing at each other, the wife tugging on the husband's arm.

"They're on the way," she whined. "Listen! They're almost here."

"Taking too long," the husband snapped. "Get in the fucking car. We can get him to the hospital before they get their thumbs outta their asses and get here."

"No, listen, Barry, they're right down the street. For fuck's sake, just listen!"

This close, Loshak could see the kid's head lolling over

the husband's forearm, the back of his skull flattened and dripping, neck obviously broken. There was nothing the ambulance would be able to do to fix him. He was gone.

"Get in the fucking car, or I'm leaving you behind," the husband said. "You're wasting precious time."

The parents must've been in shock. Unable to process the reality here, the harsh truth staring them in the face.

Loshak knew all about harsh realities. Spinks, too.

And for a second all those old feelings came over him. Watching Shelly die. Burying the dog's head. All of his shots going high, Zakarian disappearing into the pines just after. And now this fresh corpse, wrapped in a blanket, clutched in his father's arms.

But no. The past was over. Loshak couldn't touch it anymore, and it couldn't touch him.

He had to keep going. Had to.

He put the heel of his hand along his holster just to feel the cool of the gun against his skin.

He'd keep going, keep flailing against the void until he'd spent all of himself, until there was nothing left.

Neighbors from across the street were running to the parents, stopping the husband, pulling him back to the grass, away from the line of parked vehicles, trying to talk him into waiting as if the paramedics could undo death.

Red and blue lights flashed behind Loshak. He kept jogging.

Down the street, three men in their twenties were prowling around, searching for something. His gut lurched, and he sped up, ignoring the stitch under his ribs.

"Did he come through here?" Loshak hollered at them.

One with a flat-billed trucker cap spun around

aggressively. But when he saw Loshak, his shoulders dropped, and the scowl eased.

"Cop?" he asked.

Loshak nodded, slowing to a stop in front of the kid.

"He went that way." Pointing down the street. "The guy, that fucking killer from the news. He was right down there, then he disappeared. Just fucking gone."

Loshak loped off in the direction they pointed, stepping up onto the sidewalk. His knees protested the return to running, but he could see it now, on the sidewalk.

Blood.

Up ahead, it veered off down a driveway that ended in a chain link fence.

And past the fence, a shed.

CHAPTER 55

With trembling hands, Zakarian reached into his pocket and pulled out the plastic lighter. His fingers were cold and numb, so it took a couple tries before he could flick the wheel enough to get a flame.

The blood had soaked the thigh of his jeans. He could hear it pouring down his leg in sheets, squishing in his shoe. He ripped off his shirt and pressed it to the wound, trying to dam the river of red pouring out of him. Not good.

It wasn't fair. This wasn't how it worked. He was strong. Invincible. He'd proven that. Over and over and over again with the sharp end of his knife, he'd proved his strength.

He wasn't the one who was supposed to bleed.

There was a sound outside the shed. A slow swishing. Like footsteps creeping through grass, trying to sneak up on him.

His ears perked up and fear tingled along the surface of his skin. He held his breath, listening.

Yeah, someone was definitely out there. Closing in on him.

His eyelids fluttered. He chewed his lip.

His whole body shook now, every muscle pulled tight. He couldn't move. Couldn't breathe. It was terror, huge, filling up his head, just like when he was a kid. Like all those times he knew the pain was coming, knew there was nothing he could do to escape it.

He aimed the gun at the shed door. Electricity thrummed in his fingers, ready to pull the trigger. He swallowed past the lump in his throat. Felt it bob like a fist wedged in there.

The door swung open.

CHAPTER 56

Loshak hauled open the shed door, orange streetlight pouring into the gap, illuminating the darkness. And there he was. Edward Zakarian. The killer, the monster who had just smashed a little boy's head in less than two hundred yards away, now slumped against the wall and covered in blood.

Eyes wide enough to show their whites even in the strange orange-black glow locked on Loshak's face. In person Loshak saw none of the dark pitted look to them, none of the shadowy effect he'd seen in all of the photos. Christ, he looked like a boy up close. Scrawny and baby-faced.

"I surrender!" Zakarian whimpered. His voice was small, thin. Whiny. A child on the verge of tears.

He threw the gun at Loshak's feet and put his hands up, mirroring the posture Loshak had taken earlier in the parking lot.

"Please!" the killer sniveled. "I give up! Please!"

Hatred thrummed in Loshak's veins, lighting his vision up in shades of burning red. Here this kid was screaming for mercy while down the street a dad cradled his son's broken head in his arms.

Loshak didn't hesitate. Didn't have to think about it.

He took a step forward, pointed his gun at Zakarian's face and squeezed the trigger. Three times in quick succession.

261

The sound of the gunfire echoed off the shed walls with a splitting metallic crack. Ringing. Shivering. The sound of the night torn open wide.

Blood and brain and bits of skull spattered the back wall of the shed, droplets streaking down the window in slow motion.

CHAPTER 57

Loshak's arm fell to his side. He tucked his Glock back into the holster out of habit, snapping it absently.

But he didn't move out of the doorway.

He felt this strange whooshing in his stomach and chest, a crackling heat. A fire raging out of control. Spreading. Swelling. Flushing his face. Burning behind his eyes, drying them out.

It was over. The killer was dead.

But the anger wouldn't let up. It felt like a bonfire someone had thrown dry brush and diesel fuel on. It was burning hot and for the long haul.

The moaning sound of sirens managed to break through the brushfire. They didn't seem to be getting any closer.

So he just stood there, staring down at the bloody smear on the back wall of the shed. Fists clenching and unclenching.

And pressure built in his skull. Hatred boiling. Words and thoughts lost in the seething squall, turning to dark colors and indistinct shapes.

He wasn't sure how much time had passed when he heard footsteps approaching the shed.

"The guys back there said you went this way..." Spinks' voice trailed off, and the footsteps came to a stop.

Loshak realized his chest was heaving, air hissing and wheezing in and out through his nose like some overweight, apnea-ridden bulldog. His jaw ached from gritting his teeth. Embarrassed to be caught this way — to have somebody witness him like this — he swallowed hard and tried to calm his ragged breathing. And blink. He couldn't remember blinking since he pulled the trigger. His eyes burned.

Spinks stepped into the shed next to him, pressing a wadded piece of blood-soaked cloth to his shoulder. The reporter opened his mouth and inhaled, ready to say something, but he let it back out.

Loshak followed his gaze to the body sprawled against the back wall of the shed, the broken skull lolling atop the limp, skeletal figure. The blood seeped slowly outward from the body, the rounded puddle crawling over the cement slab in slow motion.

Spinks tore his eyes away from it and turned to Loshak. "You all right?" he asked.

Loshak glanced at the reporter from the corner of his eye. Nodded. He didn't think he could manage to vocalize anything yet.

After a few seconds' silence, Spinks gestured at the discarded handgun at their feet.

"So, he pointed his gun at you, and you shot him, right? That's what happened?"

Loshak felt his breathing kick up again. He tried to wrestle it back under control but couldn't.

Spinks kicked the gun with the side of his shoe, half scooting it across the floor. It skidded over the cement and into the pool of blood, coming to rest near the killer's limp, white hand.

"Yeah," Spinks said, nodding. "That's what happened."

EPILOGUE

Two weeks after things wrapped up in Florida, Loshak made the three-hour drive down from Quantico to Norfolk. It was Monday afternoon, a strategically chosen time slot. Jan was staying there with her sister Annette, and Annette had Mah Jong club on Mondays.

There wasn't any bad blood between Loshak and Annette, but the feelings weren't all hunky-dory, either. His former sister-in-law had been the sympathetic shoulder Jan cried on while her husband chased down criminals and tried not to think about his daughter's death. Not his finest hour for an audience. For his part, Loshak hadn't been too crazy about coming home to find Annette helping Jan sort through the divorce papers she'd been about to present him. Maybe it went both ways to a certain degree.

No bad blood, but plenty of unpleasant memories. Better to avoid dredging them up.

Loshak turned down the quiet cul-de-sac, pulled into the brick-lined crescent drive of number 5226, and parked off to the side, leaving plenty of room just in case Annette came home early. For a while he sat in the car staring at the windows of the snug little brick cottage with its hunter green front door and matching shutters. Wondering if Jan was standing behind those gauzy curtains staring out at his car.

With a wry laugh, Loshak realized he was nervous. It

265

wasn't like this was a date. He'd promised to visit while she was up here, and this was him following through on that promise. And bringing a little surprise. He grabbed the newspaper Spinks had sent him via snail-mail, "just in case you want to frame it." News articles were strictly gifts of friendship. Roses, now that would've been date material.

He climbed out and shut the car door behind him, flinching internally at the way the thud echoed down the quiet street, announcing his arrival to the whole neighborhood. Made him feel that much more self-conscious. He stuck the newspaper under his arm and headed up the walk.

The front door opened before he made it to the top step. Jan appeared in the gap, that warm smile lighting up her face. Loshak stopped where he stood, one foot on the bottom step, the other on the top, a sudden ache in his chest. With her hair pulled back, and the sweatshirt and jeans on, she looked like the smart-mouthed grad student he'd proposed to all those years ago.

Then she was hugging him and saying, "I can't believe you drove all the way down here. Come inside, come inside. The—"

"Front step is no place for reunions," he said, all anxiety dropping away. "I know."

She stepped inside, holding the door open for him to follow.

"Well, I know the first thing I'd want to hear after a three-hour drive." She pointed down the hall to their left. "Bathroom's that way. First door on the left. You remember."

"Yeah, thanks." He held out the paper, folded open to

display the article in question. "Before I forget, this is for you. 'Coral Gables Man Returning from Vacation Arrested with 3lbs Cocaine in Rectum'."

Her brows scrunched together as she took it, eyes studying the mugshot of a certain psychotic landlord beneath the headline.

While Jan read, Lohsak excused himself to the bathroom. When he came back, she glanced up at him.

"This is why he was always flying down to Mexico? Son of a bitch was keistering cocaine?" she asked.

Loshak shrugged. "Maybe he was trying to pay off those fines and back taxes."

He'd expected her to get a laugh out of the article — he had — but she was frowning down at the paper.

"You'd think with all the news segments on airport security that most people would be smarter than to bring drugs in on commercial flights," she said.

"Most, probably," Loshak agreed. "Just not this genius."

Jan just shook her head, still staring down at the mugshot.

"Spinks said he didn't have time to get it in before printing, but they sentenced Seidel to six years," Loshak said.

He felt stupid for pushing it, but a small part of him wanted to show his ex-wife that the asshole who'd terrorized her all those months had gotten what he deserved. That he was off the streets and locked away.

She deflated a little as the air left her lungs.

"It doesn't bring her back," she said. Almost whispered.

Loshak wasn't sure whether Jan was talking about her little dog or Shelly. Or maybe both. He didn't want to ask.

Didn't want to tear either wound open if the landlord's embarrassing arrest wasn't going to do anything to help close it.

"Well, hell," he said, rubbing the back of his neck. "I guess next time I'll skip the paper and bring you flowers instead."

Jan tucked a stray hair behind her ear and smiled, a hint of pink creeping in along the edges of her jaw.

"I wouldn't say no to that," she said.

THANK YOU

Thanks so much for reading *Beyond Good & Evil*! Want another Loshak novel? Leave a review on Amazon and let us know.

A NOTE FROM THE AUTHORS

Unfortunately, Edward Zakarian's crimes were based on true events, albeit loosely. We researched a couple of real serial killers in excruciating depth before we put this one together, scared the daylights out of ourselves, put our own spin on said events, and turned it into the book you've just read.

Still, as dark as it was, *Beyond Good & Evil* was fun to write. Maybe that sounds strange. Maybe it is strange. I don't know.

As we work on finishing it up and prepare to send out into the world, I can't help but wonder if it will be fun to read. Maybe fun is the wrong word here.

There is something exciting about staring into the darkness without blinking, without flinching, something striking and visceral and strange. It hurts sometimes, and it's terrifying most of the time, but it always makes me feel more alive. That's what working on this one was like for me, and fun is about the best word I can come up with for it.

So you've read it. What do you think: Are we having fun yet?

Kalamazoo, Michigan
September 16, 2018

MORE LOSHAK

But wait! How will you find out about more Loshak?

It's a sad fact that Amazon won't magically beam news of upcoming Loshak books into your head. (I wish.) Don't miss out! Choose one of the options below to keep up with Loshak, Jan, and Spinks:

1) You can join our Facebook Fan group. Then you'll hear all about our new and upcoming releases. Join at: **http://facebook.com/groups/mcbainvargus**

2) You can follow us on Amazon. Just go to one of our author pages and click on the FOLLOW button under our pictures. That way Amazon will send you an email whenever we publish something new.

3) You can join the E.M. Smith mailing list. In fact, we'll give you a free copy of the next book in the Loshak series (a short) if you partake in this one. Just visit: **http://ltvargus.com/emfreebook**

See where it all started for Loshak in the *Violet Darger* series...

Her body is broken. Wrapped in plastic. Dumped on the side of the road. She is the first. There will be more.

The serial killer thriller that "refuses to let go until you've read the last sentence."

The most recent body was discovered in the grease dumpster behind a Burger King. Dismembered. Shoved into two garbage bags and lowered into the murky oil.

Now rookie agent **Violet Darger** gets the most important assignment of her career. She travels to the Midwest to face a killer unlike anything she's seen. Aggressive. Territorial. Deranged and driven.

Another mutilated corpse was found next to a roller rink. A third in the gutter in a residential neighborhood.

These bold displays of violence shock the rural community and rattle local law enforcement.

Who could carry out such brutality? And why?

Unfortunately for Agent Darger, there's little physical evidence to work with, and the only witnesses prove to be unreliable. The case seems hopeless.

If she fails, more will die. He will kill again and again.

The victims harbor dark secrets. The clues twist and writhe and refuse to keep still. And the killer watches the investigation on the nightly news, gleeful to relive the violence, knowing that he can't be stopped.

Get your copy now: **http://mybook.to/DeadEndGirl**

ABOUT THE AUTHORS

E.M. Smith came by his redneck roots honestly, his barbwire tattoo dishonestly, and his sobriety slowly. Recovery isn't a sprint, according to his friends, it's a marathon. That's probably why he turned into such a fitness geek when he quit drinking.

L.T. Vargus grew up in Hell, Michigan, which is a lot smaller, quieter, and less fiery than one might imagine. When not glued to her computer, she can be found sewing, fantasizing about food, and rotting her brain in front of the TV.

    If you want to wax poetic about pizza or cats, you can contact L.T. (the L is for Lex) at ltvargus9@gmail.com or on Twitter @ltvargus.

Tim McBain writes because life is short, and he wants to make something awesome before he dies. Additionally, he likes to move it, move it.

    You can connect with Tim via email at tim@timmcbain.com.